Gabriela Houston

THE WIND CHILD

Illustrated by Alexis Snell

uclanpublishing

HAVE YOU EVER WONDERED HOW BOOKS ARE MADE?

UCLan Publishing is an award winning independent publisher specialising in Children's and Young Adult books. Based at The University of Central Lancashire, this Preston-based publisher teaches MA Publishing students how to become industry professionals using the content and resources from its business; students are included at every stage of the publishing process and credited for the work that they contribute.

The business doesn't just help publishing students though. UCLan Publishing has supported the employability and real-life work skills for the University's Illustration, Acting, Translation, Animation, Photography, Film & TV students and many more. This is the beauty of books and stories; they fuel many other creative industries! The MA Publishing students are able to get involved from day one with the business and they acquire a behind the scenes experience of what it is like to work for a such a reputable independent.

The MA course was awarded a Times Higher Award (2018) for Innovation in the Arts and the business, UCLan Publishing, was awarded Best Newcomer at the Independent Publishing Guild (2019) for the ethos of teaching publishing using a commercial publishing house. As the business continues to grow, so too does the student experience upon entering this dynamic Masters course.

www.uclanpublishing.com
www.uclanpublishing.com/courses/
uclanpublishing@uclan.ac.uk

CREATURES AND GODS

- **Stribog** – God of Winter Winds, Music and Silver
- **Zevena** – Daughter of Stribog, a minor wind spirit
- **Dogoda** – Brother of Stribog, father of the three Zoryas, God of Summer Winds
- **Zorya Yutrenna-ya** – Daughter of Dogoda, Goddess of the Morning
- **Zorya Vecherna-ya** – Daughter of Dogoda, Goddess of the Evening
- **Zorya Necna-ya** – Daughter of Dogoda, Goddess of the Night
- **Sudiki** – The three sisters in the Veeray Tree, Goddesses of Fate and the guardians of the Root Souls
- **Veles** – The trickster God of Navia, the afterlife, and the God of the Sea
- **Vila** – The Goddess of Lightning
- **Upior** – a demonic ghost
- **Stigoi** – a demon with two hearts, preying on travellers
- **Gamayun** – A half bird/half woman
- **Kania** – a female demon who kidnaps lost children
- **Viaterce** – Wind demons
- **Vodyanoi** – Water spirits
- **Rusalki** – Female water demons, who drown men foolish enough to approach in to the water

- ☀ **Dusiol** – A malicious demon which saps the life and health from its victims
- ☀ **Heidash** – A minor demon with the head and legs of a ram
- ☀ **Viatroduya** – One of Stribog's many children. A malicious wind sprite
- ☀ **Borovy and Borova** – The Guardians of the Forests
- ☀ **Baba Latingorka** – A powerful shape-shifting witch guarding the Alatnir
- ☀ **Lubac the Serpent** – A monster snake
- ☀ **Koschei the Deathless** – An immortal creature who hides its soul within the stone Alatnir

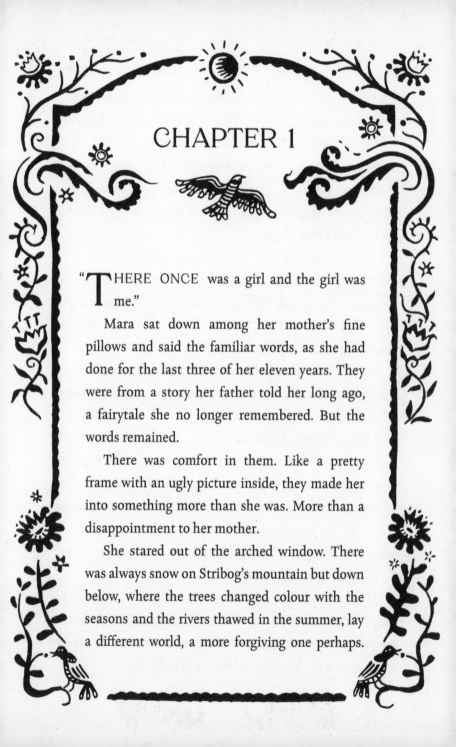

CHAPTER 1

"THERE ONCE was a girl and the girl was me."

Mara sat down among her mother's fine pillows and said the familiar words, as she had done for the last three of her eleven years. They were from a story her father told her long ago, a fairytale she no longer remembered. But the words remained.

There was comfort in them. Like a pretty frame with an ugly picture inside, they made her into something more than she was. More than a disappointment to her mother.

She stared out of the arched window. There was always snow on Stribog's mountain but down below, where the trees changed colour with the seasons and the rivers thawed in the summer, lay a different world, a more forgiving one perhaps.

The towns and the villages of Prissan were just about visible over the horizon, the colour of them drained over the distance, so they all seemed grey and blue to Mara's eyes.

Mara looked at her mother, bustling about in her shimmering beauty. Zevena's skin was light blue, like a frosted-over forget-me-not, and so bright it hurt if you looked at it for too long.

But Mara's skin was the unremarkable white of skin bereft of the sun; of uncooked dough; of her human father's tired eyes, lined with small pink veins. Her eyes were light brown, like his, and her hair was a mousy brown, its two plaits falling down her back.

If Mara waited long enough, every now and again Zevena would stop what she was doing and would pet her daughter's head in an absent-minded way.

Like you'd pet a half-feral cat.

It was as if her mother was saying, "Such a surprise to see you here. I don't expect you to stay." Mara could see the confusion in her mother's eyes every time they chanced to pause on her daughter's face, yet she stayed, not knowing what else to do with herself, aside from sitting in this room by her dozing father.

How different it was when Yaris, Mara's father, her beloved da, was well. He'd take her hunting with him, nearly every time he went, and he used to go nearly every day. He'd go to escape the boredom of Mara's grandfather's icy palace,

or perhaps to escape Zevena; Mara wasn't sure. Perhaps it was just that he liked to feel the cold air pinch his cheeks once more, to remind him he was alive.

All Mara knew was she loved those times, sitting in front of him on his ageing black pony, so different from her mother's almost unnaturally well-behaved silver palfrey. He brought his pony with him when he came to live with her mother, and loved that animal, for the same reason Zevena would wrinkle her nose at it. It was small and fat and ungainly, and solid in a way no other creature in Stribog's palace was. When Mara rode on it with her father she would lean forward and inhale its earthy smell, letting her small ungloved hands run over its silky neck, moist with perspiration.

"Look, *Marushka!*" her father would sometimes say, and he'd point to a track in the snow or to a shape moving between the trees. He'd always hold Mara with one hand, though they both knew she could hold onto the saddle well enough.

But that was before. Before he began spending each day in the fur-covered bed, colour draining from his face. At first Mara searched for the cut, for the place where all her da's colour and his blood must have been draining away, leaving him almost as pale as the covers he lay on. She could see his pain when he tried to smile for her sake. They both knew she needed those smiles. They were the only ones Mara got in the House of the Winds.

Now she smiled at him from the edge of the bed where she sat. His eyelids fluttered and he stroked her shoulder, then let his hand fall away as if the effort exhausted him. Mara reached out and squeezed his hand. Soon he'd get better and they'd go out on an adventure again. Ride out till they reached the green grass and the leafy trees with their ripe nuts and pinecones filled with sweet little seeds.

Mara's grandfather blew into the room through the shutterless window, startling her.

"Good day, grandfather," Mara said, as was expected. Stribog didn't deign to respond as he assumed his human form. He hardly ever did, though Mara knew he'd be angry if she forgot those little pleasantries herself.

"Father," Zevena curtsied. Mara had tried to imitate the movement before, in front of a large mirror, and found it impossibly ridiculous. She had looked like a metal spring bobbing up and down. Her mother made it elegant.

"It is kind of you to join us," Zevena said. Mara arched an eyebrow. She severely doubted it. Stribog, like all his wind kin, was seldom considerate and never kind.

Yaris turned in his bed to face Stribog but said nothing. Their relationship was strained at the best of times.

Stribog's features flowed and shifted till their form pleased him. He pointed at Mara. "I have come to a decision." Mara pricked up her ears. "The three of you will travel to Yaris' human kin. It's only right Mara's human grandmother

have Yaris in his final days, and for Mara to grow among them till she no longer needs her mother."

Mara looked at him confused.

"Last days of what?" she asked. Could Stribog really mean it? Would she be allowed to leave his palace at last? A shiver of excitement ran down her spine. Once with his family, her da would recover and they would explore that new world together. The world which changed with the seasons and where she wasn't the most powerless of all she met. She beamed at her da, who didn't seem as excited as she'd hoped.

Her grandfather's long beard twisted into frost patterns as he pursed his lips, then blew a stronger breeze through her hair in an icy caress. Mara suspected he thought it was something grandfathers did but she wished he wouldn't. It felt like being plunged into icy water. Mara wondered briefly what it'd have been like to be the granddaughter of Stribog's younger brother, Dogoda, the God of Summer Winds. Would the warmth in that home extend beyond the weather, or would her great-uncle's island be as lonely as Stribog's icy palace? Zevena's voice brought Mara back.

"But I can't leave here ..." Zevena stood up. "My place is with you, father."

"Your place is by the daughter you chose to bear. And her place is not here." The human features Stribog wore that day faded in and out of view with every breath, but his piercing

blue eyes remained, their glare suspended in the air, fixed on Zevena. Mara's grandfather kept his eyes on his daughter and never once looked at Yaris. Mara thought it was because he found him difficult and was glad of an excuse to be rid of him. She didn't mind what Stribog said of her. She was born in his palace, but she didn't belong in it, as she was often reminded. Her lack of powers and her lack of beauty. Her lack of wit and, most disappointingly, her lack of magic. Mara was defined by the lack of all the things she should have been. And her mother was shamed by it.

"She won't need me when she's with her folk." Zevena was persistent. Yaris shot her a reproachful look which she ignored.

Stribog turned to Mara. He said nothing and she realised what he wanted her to say.

"I still need her," she said. Her da smiled at her and nodded, even as her mother balled her hands into fists.

"And so you shall have her," her grandfather said before leaving.

"You did well to claim your ma," her da said that night, as she snuggled next to him in her parents' large bed. "Zevena is your mother and you need each other, though she doesn't understand it. But I believe she loved me once and if she could love you, perhaps that would be something to keep your roots to the ground, little *zabka*."

She nodded like she understood.

"You are my roots, da," she said.

Her father smiled and brushed a strand of hair off Mara's forehead. His hand was thin and the skin on it near-translucent. She would know this hand to be his though, no matter how thin and sickly it got. She knew the hair on his fingers and the freckle on his knuckle and the shape of his long oval nails. She had little to love in her grandfather's palace: a little tune played before meals in the great hall; the robin which fluttered to her window every morning for the crumbs she'd lay out; her soft feather bed with the curtains around it to make her feel safe. Above all the wonders in Stribog's palace, Mara loved her father best of all.

The road to Mara's grandmother's house was long, but comfortable. Yaris insisted on bringing his old pony with them, and every now and again Mara would reach out from the side of the *voz* to stroke the animal's warm side. It was old and tired, too tired for the journey, in truth, but it clung to life. Mara thought maybe her da felt sympathy for his old mount: sick, just as he was. Tired just as he was ... *No*. Mara shook her head. She would banish those thoughts.

Stribog had sent them on their way with an entourage worthy of his glory. Their journey through the snow was lit up by hundreds of ice moths, their luminescent wings filling the forest with a soft hum, warning the *upiors* and the *strigas* that the family of the God of Winter Winds was coming, and they would do well to stay out of sight.

Viatroduya, one of Stribog's many wind spirit children, was charged with checking the road ahead, and every now and again Mara could hear his annoyed whistling, as he clearly thought such a charge beneath him. He'd not dared disobey Stribog though. None of them would.

Mara and her da were set up comfortably on one of the three large horse-drawn *vozy*. The *vozy* were beautiful but moved slowly, so as not to jiggle them around, and Mara wished for a whip she could crack in the air to make the sharp-toothed horses pulling them pick up the pace. At least she and Yaris were warm, snuggled under the thick furs. Her mother, of course, needed no such comforts. Zevena sat rigid and still in her gauzy gown, a high *kokoshnik* of silver and sapphires spilling its treasures on her forehead and around her face, the long beaded strands of sparkling jewels trailing down her bare neck.

Zevena looked regal and beautiful, just as she'd intended. She was staring straight ahead, a blank look on her face. Mara knew it hurt her mother to leave Stribog's domain, though she tried not to show it. Mara's grandfather travelled where he willed, but not so his daughters. His icy offspring seldom ventured outside of the palace compound. Of course her mother had done so once, years ago, and brought Yaris back with her, like a souvenir, a trophy from an adventure.

Mara was an unexpected, unwelcome surprise. Years ago, Zevena had told her daughter she suspected Stribog had breathed vitality into her frozen womb, so that she'd be punished for her dalliance with Yaris. It didn't bother Mara too much that Zevena considered her a punishment, because she knew, to her father, she was a gift.

Branches domed over the path, obscuring the sky. Only now and again did Mara catch sight of a sliver of the moon's crescent. She counted the number of times she spotted it, leaning against her father's warm shoulder: *One. Two. Three…*

The horses whinnied as the procession stopped abruptly, with the drivers pulling hard of the reigns. Mara nearly fell from her seat.

"What's the matter?" Yaris called out.

Zevena stood up, and clicked her fingers, blue flame rising high above her hand, lighting the shadow perched on the branch above them.

"Gamayun," she said, her voice devoid of emotion.

"Zevena." The creature sitting above them replied. Mara

squinted. Gamayun's face and torso were that of a woman, though much larger than that of any human woman Mara had ever seen. The rest of the body was that of an eagle, with clawed feet leaving sap-wet tracks on the branch where they tore through the bark like butter.

Mara pressed against her father. But then she looked at Zevena, sitting up tall and fearless, and was instantly ashamed of her own childish fear. She straightened up and forced herself to look up at Gamayun. The bird woman locked eyes with her and smiled. Her bare arms, muscled like a man's, were folded nonchalantly over her chest. She had a handsome face, with an owlish look around the eyes, perhaps. Mara found herself smiling. There was something akin to recognition in Gamayun's expression.

Zevena noticed and frowned.

"What do you want, Gamayun? We still have far to go, and my daughter and her father are human and susceptible to the night's dangers."

Gamayun moved her taloned feet along the branch. "Koschei the Deathless is in your path. Find a different way."

Zevena stiffened slightly. "We have no business with Koschei. No quarrel with him either."

"Your child is quarrel enough," Gamayun said, looking at Mara. *Gauging my reaction*, Mara thought – so she showed none.

"Koschei dislikes half things, and though he might not go

out of his way to break what's out of his sight, like a cat with a vase within its reach, he can't resist giving a slight *push*."

Zevena looked at Mara and bit her lip. "Stribog wouldn't allow it."

Gamayun laughed. "Stribog banished you to live with the humans. There's hardly a living thing up and down the Veeray tree who hasn't heard and laughed at Zevena the Proud's exile. Stribog wouldn't raise a finger. And Koschei has his own history with you, the least of Stribog's children, doesn't he?"

"What does she mean?" Yaris, who had hitherto been silent, asked.

Zevena didn't bother turning towards him. "An old tale from before your grandfather grew a beard, Yaris." To Gamayun she said, "Why did you bother coming to warn me? What do you care what happens to me and mine?"

Gamayun spread her wings. "Half things are Koschei's to loathe and mine to protect. And I like you owing me."

"Your Masters have sent you, haven't they?" Zevena raised an eyebrow.

Gamayun bristled slightly but nodded an acknowledgement. She jumped off the branch and swooped so close by Mara's *voz*, she brushed against the girl's hair with the tip of her wing. Then she flew away, till she was no more than a shadow against the moon.

Zevena sat down heavily. "Turn the horses," she called

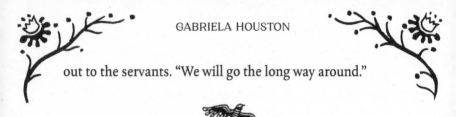

out to the servants. "We will go the long way around."

After that they travelled in silence, each comfortable with their own thoughts.

Mara sat opposite her mother, snuggled next to Yaris. She could hear his raspy breathing and put her small hands over his. He smiled at her and she thought, for certain, the family that had brought him up must be so filled with love, its force alone would cure him.

She had never met her human grandmother. When Mara was still small, her mother wished her ever close to the palace, expecting that some of its magic would rub off on her. No excursions beyond the lands of Stribog were allowed, though Yaris often bent the rules in his excursions with Mara. But as Mara's hair and then her eyes turned brown, Zevena had lost all hope her daughter might display any gifts of her divine side of the family.

It took them all the next day and the better part of the night to reach her grandmother's gates. It was still dark when they arrived, and there were few sounds, as even the most early-rising farm animals were still sound asleep. Yaris' mother lived with his brother and his family in a big homestead on the edge of the village. They were wealthy by village standards, with pigs, geese, chickens and a cow or two to help fend off starvation even in the deepest winters, which was saying a lot.

One of Stribog's servants jumped off the first *voz* and pushed the creaky gate open. A dog barked in the house and after a moment a light appeared in the window. Zevena frowned at Mara, who, heedless of the servant's outstretched hand, jumped off the *voz* herself. Mara didn't care. She was eager to see her first chicken!

The door opened and a bearded face looked out. The man squinted through the dark. "Who goes there?" he called out, fear in his voice.

"It's me, Gnievos," Yaris said, in a voice so low, his brother clearly didn't hear him.

"Show yourself!" the man called out again.

Mara's da, with the help of two servants, got off the *voz*, and hobbled, half-carried, towards the light.

Gnievos' eyes narrowed for a moment in a short-sighted sort of way as he struggled to see.

The change was sudden and dramatic. Blood drained from his face and his hands fell by his side.

"Who is it, Gnievos? Why are you standing there like a calf staring at a painted gate? No thought in your head, just—" An old woman pushed her way past Gnievos and, leaning on a stick, hobbled across the porch. She shoved the candle she was holding into her son's hand and looked straight at Mara's party, letting her eyes adjust to the dark.

"*Mamusha*, it's me ..." Yaris' voice broke.

Mara felt a ball rise up in her own throat. She imagined being reunited with her own da after such a long absence and thought she could understand how he felt. She felt a surge of as-yet-unearned love for her grandmother, for the woman who could make her father's voice break.

". . . Yaris?" Her grandmother walked another step. "Yaris! My boy!" She moved with a speed which belied her age and was met halfway by her son, who seemed to have reserved some strength just for this reunion. They wrapped their arms around each other and both sank to their knees, crying and laughing.

This surprised Mara. She'd never seen an adult cry before. She didn't know they could.

Her uncle, Gnievos, found his voice now and called out to the rest of the family in the house. They poured out of the door, a seemingly endless procession of brown-eyed faces. Gnievos ran towards Mara's father and his mother and held them tight.

Through it all Mara stood apart, next to Zevena, who remained unnoticed, in spite of her splendor. The servants were already unloading the *vozy*, the many possessions grabbing the attention of several children who wriggled out of their mother's arms to investigate the silver-lined coffers and touch the soft folded furs with their small hands. One of Stribog's servants smiled at the child closest to him, who squealed and ran to his mother. The servant shrugged his shoulders. A *latavietz*'s rows of teeth were as everyday to Mara as her breakfast bowl, but it began to dawn on her that her normal was less than ordinary to these children, barefoot one and all, heedless of the snow on the ground.

Mara longed to approach them and introduce herself but her mother lay a hand on her shoulder. Zevena straightened herself further, which Mara wouldn't have thought possible a moment before, and said in a voice which carried straight to the mind of those around, "I am Zevena Stribogovna, the daughter of the God of Winter Winds, and the mother of your son's child."

Yaris' family all snapped their heads towards Zevena, who pushed Mara gently forward, like some kind of offering. Mara watched the surprise in their eyes. She didn't blame them. It seemed impossible that this blue-skinned goddess could claim her as her own.

Yaris nodded towards his daughter, not letting go of his mother's shoulders. "*Mamusha*," he said, breathless, and Mara's mouth gaped open at the tear-tracks down his cheeks. "This is my little girl, Mara Gontovna, my dearest *Marushka*. I know you will care for her as I do, for you will not find a child easier to love."

Yaris' mother looked at her son's feverish, eager face, and then turned to Mara. She was the oldest human Mara had ever seen, with deep grooves running across her paper-thin skin. Her face was round and her eyebrows were perfect crescents above her thoughtful brown eyes, giving her a slightly surprised look. Sorona Gontova reluctantly let go of her son and hobbled over to Mara. She grunted with effort as she bent down to bring her face in front of her granddaughter's, before placing her hands on Mara's cheeks and kissing her on the lips. "*Marushka*, I'm so happy to meet you, child. You look just like your father." A thought struck Sorona and she turned a fearful expression towards Mara's mother. "No offence meant, Zevena Stribogovna, but this child does not bear the gods' mark to an old woman's eye."

Zevena gave a stiff little bow with her head, acknowledging the old woman's words.

Sorona looked back at Yaris, her hand brushing away an errant curl off her son's forehead. "Are you all back here for good? Is my family complete again?"

Yaris tried to smile. "Such as it is, mother, for as long as it is."

CHAPTER 2

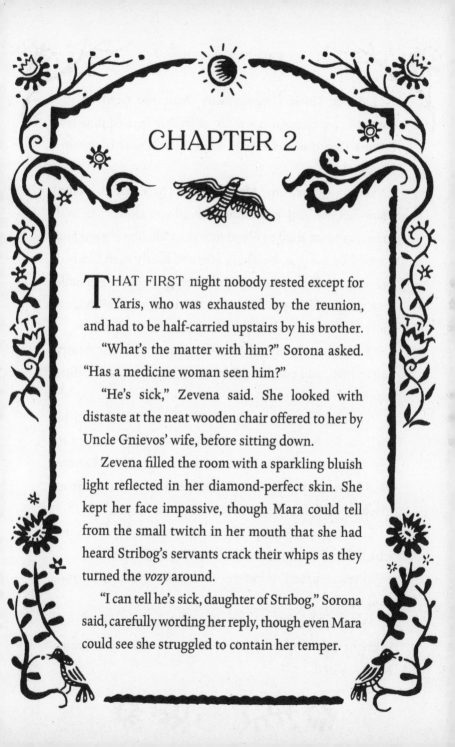

THAT FIRST night nobody rested except for Yaris, who was exhausted by the reunion, and had to be half-carried upstairs by his brother.

"What's the matter with him?" Sorona asked. "Has a medicine woman seen him?"

"He's sick," Zevena said. She looked with distaste at the neat wooden chair offered to her by Uncle Gnievos' wife, before sitting down.

Zevena filled the room with a sparkling bluish light reflected in her diamond-perfect skin. She kept her face impassive, though Mara could tell from the small twitch in her mouth that she had heard Stribog's servants crack their whips as they turned the *vozy* around.

"I can tell he's sick, daughter of Stribog," Sorona said, carefully wording her reply, though even Mara could see she struggled to contain her temper.

Balinka, Uncle Gnievos' wife, bent her head as she passed her mother-in-law a cup of freshly brewed pine tea. Sorona Gontova was clearly more than respected in this household.

Sorona turned to Mara. "Come here, child, come, *Marushka*, let your grandmother hold you close," she said to her, as Mara tried to blend into the wall. She obeyed and kneeled by her grandmother's seat and barely even flinched as Sorona ran her wizened fingers through her hair. Her nails were rough and they pulled at Mara's hair, but the child didn't move. Stillness was an important skill in Stribog's palace.

"I ask what ails my son. He disappeared a healthy, hearty young man, and you bring him to me weak and old before his time."

"He came to *me* a human," Zevena said, and you'd be forgiven for believing this was all of very little concern to her. "He comes back a human. Humans get sick. Humans die. I know only gods, who do neither of those things. So as to what he's dying of . . . I have no answers for you."

Sorona pursed her lips. There was anger in her eyes, a fire which didn't seem to scare Mara's icy mother one bit.

Zevena turned to Mara. "I would speak with you, daughter."

Mara nodded. They left the house, heedless of how rude it might have appeared to the Gontov family. *Her* family, Mara realised.

Once the door shut behind them, Zevena turned to her, the wind blowing her long braids around her shoulders.

"You have a family here, Mara. A grandmother who is clearly glad to see you. Do you need me?" There was an urgency in her look. The *vozy* were not far, the snow-covered mountain of Zevena's home loomed in the distance.

There was the pervading smell of slightly soured milk and the unpleasant stench of the chickens still sleeping in their coop. A dog barked and a baby cried inside.

Nothing like the home of Stribog.

"I still need you," Mara said.

Zevena nodded, her lips drawn to a line. A little of her light seemed to leave her, and her shoulders sagged. She walked past Mara and once more entered Sorona Gontova's house.

The morning arrived with a slew of neighbours, as the tale of Yaris' magical return with his goddess wife spread through the village like wildfire. Many were eager to see Mara's father, but her grandmother would inform most that Yaris was not well and was not to be disturbed. She made the exception for a tall lanky widower, who came in with his son, both breathless like they'd run the whole way.

"Sorona Gontova, I came as soon as I heard! Is it truly him?" said the widower, taking off his woollen hat in respect.

He kneaded it in his hands like it was dough, and didn't even notice Sorona's long-coated cat, as it batted at the string of his belt.

"Yes, Litnev, it's him, though he's tired and sick. The gods have returned him to us, not quite as they found him." Sorona brought a hand to her mouth as soon as the words escaped it and cast a fearful glance at Zevena, who pretended not to hear, sitting regally as the village women surrounded her, admiring her *kokoshnik* and her cornflower skin. Sorona shook her head, ever so slightly.

"*Mamusha*, Yaris stirred." Uncle Gnievos came down the wooden steps. "He heard Litnev's voice and is asking for him." Litnev looked at Sorona, wordlessly asking her permission.

She nodded. "You think I can say no to my son, after all these years? And when I hardly said no to him before? Go, my boy, take joy with you. He needs all he can get to grow strong again."

Litnev turned to his son. "Stay here," he said, then he bounded up the stairs, two steps at a time.

Litnev's son, a boy a year or so older than Mara, inspected her openly. She returned his gaze. She was used to being stared at. He was taller than her, but then she was small. His eyes were very big and very dark, so unlike her mother's blue and her father's light brown. The boy's hair was pure black and his skin was darker than hers.

He lifted his chin defiantly.

20

"I'm Torniv. What's your name?" He sat himself on the bench next to her, without asking. Mara wasn't sure if her mother wished her to show displeasure or not. But none of the other children had approached her, or so much as attempted to speak with her, so she smiled at the boy.

"Mara, but my friends call me *Marushka*," she said.

He raised an eyebrow at her. "Do you have many of those then?"

She glared, which only made him chuckle, but his smile disappeared when he looked up to see Zevena staring at him.

She didn't frown, she didn't even seem particularly interested in his existence. But Mara knew how that stare could make you feel, and she felt sorry for him.

When Zevena once more turned her attention to the women around her, Torniv leaned towards Mara, so close his lips nearly brushed the tip of her ear. "This can't be your ma," he said, decisively.

Mara bristled. "Of course she is!"

He shook his head. "She's a goddess and look at you! You're human, just like me."

"You don't know anything!" Mara had forgotten to whisper. She could feel her mother's cold blue eyes on her, curious, probing.

"What are you two whispering about?" Her grandmother's head was barely visible through the crowd. "*Marushka*, come to me, I would have you sit with me."

Mara nodded at Torniv stiffly, to let him know *this* wasn't finished.

She approached her grandmother. Sorona reached out for Mara's hand and stroked it with her thumb. Mara froze up. This was what she'd hoped for: this affection, this warmth. And yet, unused as she was to it, she needed a moment to process these new feelings.

"This here is my granddaughter, Mara Gontovna," Sorona said to the neighbours, who all smiled politely. Zevena's presence was felt by all like a cold shiver down their backs and, though she looked like her father, Mara suspected that all those gathered were waiting to see if she would sprout wings or grow fangs before they could relax around her.

Sorona noticed the neighbours' stiffness and she drew back her shoulders, pushing her wizened chest forward. "She is my Yaris' daughter, and she is of this house. I intend to treat her as the miracle that she is, returned to me after all these years." She looked at Mara and raised her hand to her granddaughter's cheek. Sorona stroked her skin with her hand, its rough, calloused surface scratchy, but oddly comforting.

Mara noticed, with shock, that there were tears staining her grandmother's cheek.

The neighbours must have noticed too, for they all soon made their excuses, disappointed in their hopes of seeing Mara's father, but, no doubt, comforting themselves that

the sight of Zevena would provide them with enough gossip for a while.

A few stragglers were politely ushered out by Aunt Balinka. Mara was beginning to like her uncle's wife, who seemed a quiet, no-nonsense kind of a woman. She was short, nearly as short as Mara, with a thick waist, and wide hands. Her pale blond hair peeked out from under her flowery scarf, which she kept tied under her chin. The four children in the house were hers and were kept snug and warm, wrapped in their parents' love and affection. Mara envied them.

It was early afternoon when the last of the guests had left. Litnev took the longest, and came down the stairs with his eyes red and his lips in a tight line. He whispered a few words to Sorona, too low for Mara to hear. He then nodded to Mara, after appraising her in silence for a moment.

Torniv followed him, but not before flashing a bright smile at Mara. It confused her. The boy exuded friendliness, unlike the other village children, but his comment about Mara not looking like her mother had bothered her.

"I'd better go upstairs," Sorona said, and Mara realised she must have eagerly awaited this moment. Sorona patted her on the head. "You come with me, child, let's see how your father is getting on. Our duty to the village has been done and I don't intend to leave Yaris' side tonight."

"Do you wish for Mara to be there?" Zevena asked,

looking straight ahead, so it was impossible to tell who she was asking.

Mara's grandmother tensed and said, "If you allow it, Zevena Stribogovna."

Zevena made no sign she heard, except shifting her eyes to Mara. Mara nodded, and Zevena immediately relaxed.

"I will stay here, then, until you need me," Zevena said.

Mara's grandmother raised her eyebrows quizzically but seemed happy with this answer.

Aunt Balinka offered to help her mother-in-law up, but Sorona waved her away. "*Marushka* can help me. Can't you, *moya zabka*?" Mara nodded.

Only her father had ever called her that. His *zabka*, his little froggy. Zevena once bristled at the nickname, that he would call Mara something so small and insignificant. He shook his head at Zevena then, and pulled her into his arms and kissed her, as he used to do, and said with a laugh, "She is little, and delicate, and full of life and colour. She has a lifetime to be dignified."

It felt odd to Mara for this near-stranger to call her by that name. To claim her in that way. Mara wanted to enjoy it, to relax into the feeling of being wanted, but the cold part of her pushed back at this unearned familiarity.

Mara suddenly realised her grandmother was waiting for her to answer. She nodded and Sorona leaned on her, more heavily than Mara had expected.

"Your mother is a cold one, and no mistake," Sorona said as they walked up the stairs.

Mara didn't say anything.

"Barely said more than two words to you since you arrived, or as much as enquired after your father, but then she's a god's daughter and I'm just an old woman who knows nothing of the gods' ways."

Mara concentrated on helping her grandmother up the creaky stairs. The old woman smelled like bread and apples whenever she breathed out. A strange, bodily smell. Nobody had smelled like that in Stribog's palace.

"But then you are just as silent. As is good and proper in a young girl, of course, though rare enough in a healthy and happy child."

Mara was at a loss for what she wanted from her. Did she like her silent or not? Sorona probably didn't mean it unkindly, but after Torniv's words, Mara didn't need any further lines drawn between her and her mother, so she said, "I'm her daughter as well."

Sorona eyed her strangely. "Nobody said you're not."

"Well..." Mara hesitated, not sure if she should trust this old woman, but Sorona was her grandmother after all. "That boy did. I think he didn't believe I was really my mother's daughter. Which isn't fair," she sniffed, "because it's not like she'd claim me if I wasn't."

Sorona laughed, displaying a few teeth sitting at odd

angles in her mouth. "He was getting a rise out of you, pay him no mind." She leaned her head towards Mara and paused just as they were climbing up the last step, "His ma was Botrish, and flighty, like all their kind. Litnev, his da, was torn up when she died and left him with the baby. Like a man would know what to do with one! But he seemed to understand more than most, and had the wisdom to ask advice where he didn't. And so he raised this halfling, as wild as the winds, and just as untrustworthy, if you ask me. Litnev stands by the boy, but it's a heavy burden for a man." She sniffed and shook her head in distaste. "The blood will tell, as they say."

"Do you really think so?" Mara asked in a small voice. Would the wind blood in her show itself in time? Or would she forever be like she was now? Powerless and meaningless.

But Sorona misunderstood Mara's words. She whipped her head around. "It's just what folk say, child." She put two fingers under Mara's chin and raised her small face so she could look her in the eyes. "I see your father in you. The Gontov blood is stronger than that ice running through your mother's veins. I see it in your eyes, light brown like mine were when I was your age. You're one of us and we won't let them take you from us. You're safe here."

Mara nodded because she sensed that was what was expected of her, but she wasn't sure she felt reassured by Sorona's words. It wasn't a comfort to have her mother erased

26

from her, nor to be claimed so decisively by this somebody she barely knew, no matter how kind.

They went into the bedroom where her father was resting. At the door Mara heard his laughter and her uncle's voice. Mara slipped away from her grandmother and scuttled to her father's side. She climbed into his bed, and grabbed hold of his hand, clearly to her grandmother's and Uncle Gnievos' surprise.

After a moment Uncle Gnievos burst out laughing. "She's like a wolf cub, defending her territory! Just look at your daughter, Yaris, she's practically snarling at me!" He leaned forward and ruffled her hair. Mara bared her teeth and was pleased to see a flash of fear cross her uncle's face. Small or no, she was Zevena's daughter and he would do well not to treat her like a pet. Yaris laughed though, and his brother soon joined him, though Sorona Gontova furrowed her eyebrows.

"Yaris, is this how you brought up your daughter? To bare her teeth, like an animal, at family?"

Yaris tensed. "This is new to her, *mamusha*. Give her time," he said, squeezing Mara's hand.

"In my house, children learn to behave, Yaris," Sorona shook her head, but a smile was already warming her face. "How are you feeling?"

Uncle Gnievos, seeing this was his sign to leave, said he'd go check on Aunt Balinka.

"So, *synek*?" Sorona perched on the side of Yaris' bed and stroked his cheek. "What's the matter with you?"

Mara's father's eyes darted to his daughter, quickly, but not fast enough for her to not notice the effort with which he feigned cheerfulness. "I'm already better for being home and seeing your face, *mamusha*. I expect a few days of your cooking and I will be up and about again."

"See that you are." Sorona sighed and wiped her eyes with the back of her sleeve. "So tell me, Yaris," she said, placing her son's hand between her own. "Tell me what you've been doing these eleven years and what Stribog's palace had to offer that would make you leave your own *mamusha*."

Yaris looked at his daughter, and then back at his mother, who nodded an understanding.

From then on, they spoke of many things: Yaris' life on the Stribog mountain, Mara's early years, and all the things Yaris had missed from back home. A multitude of births and deaths of people Mara didn't know and didn't have much interest in. However, nobody threw her out and so she stayed in the bed, cuddled against her father, and let his voice lull her to sleep.

A hand on Mara's shoulder woke her up. It was night already and the snow fell outside in familiar comforting swirls.

"Come, little one, we will sup together," Uncle Gnievos said. He chuckled, "Don't look at me so, child, you will soon get used to me, I promise. I'm not a picture to look at, but I love your da and will be a good friend to you."

"I believe you will be," Yaris' voice came through in a whisper. Mara whipped her head around to realise her father was awake. His expression was serious, far more than she was used to, and she didn't like the look of understanding that passed between the brothers, some message they didn't mean to include her in.

"Come with me, da," she said, pulling at Yaris' hand.

He shook his head.

Uncle Gnievos put his hand on Mara's shoulder, "Come, child, let your da rest a bit. Your Aunt Balinka will bring him the choicest morsels, you can be sure of that." His voice shook and so Mara followed him, out of curiosity more than sympathy. Who were these strange people with emotions as fast-changing and as strong as the winds and could she truly be one of them, as her grandmother had said?

The whole family was assembled in the large *izba* below, the adults seated at the long table, and the children wherever they could fit. Mara saw her four cousins, though they seemed to avoid her eyes whenever she addressed them.

"Here, *moya zabka*, sit between your mother and me," Sorona said.

Mara sat next to the silent Zevena.

A suppressed giggle from the opposite side of the table made her look up sharply. Two of her cousins stared at her, their heads close together. Mara frowned. She picked up her carved wooden spoon but another giggle made her pause. She looked down to her bowl of stew. She gasped and her spoon clattered to the floor.

Sorona raised her eyebrows. "What's the matter with you, child? You look like you've seen a ghost!"

Mara fought to compose herself. She forced a smile to her lips. "I'm just feeling tired, that's all."

"Oh, well, that's only understandable!" Aunt Balinka clasped her hands together. "You must be exhausted, you poor thing! Eat, and you'll sleep better!"

"Maybe she's too fine for our food, ma." One of Mara's cousins smiled sweetly at her mother, then cast a triumphant glance towards Mara.

A silence fell over the table. Mara narrowed her eyes then turned her face into the perfect mask of guileless surprise.

"Oh no, Aunt, this is some of the best food I have ever been served. But my stomach feels tight and I ate so much bread earlier that I really couldn't manage another bite." She held her cousin's gaze. "But I wouldn't let it go to waste. And I can see my cousins' bowls are empty already." She pushed her bowl towards her cousins. Their faces fell as they knew, just as well as Mara did, about the maggots they'd put

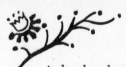

in her bowl, crawling around in a swirly mass of white.

Sorona looked at the cousins and smiled. "Well, go on then. We don't want for food in this house, but we don't waste it either."

The two kids shot Mara a hateful look but Mara noticed they did obey Sorona, raising the spoiled food to their mouths with shaking hands. Mara wondered if her grandmother suspected the trick. Either way, she doubted her cousins would try it again.

Through it all, Zevena sat very still, like a porcelain statue, apparently noticing nothing. *Useless.* Mara brought her hand to her mouth, shocked at her own thought. In Stribog's icy palace her mother had always seemed an impossible ideal, regal and distant. Here, in all her finery, among these people, she seemed out of place.

Mara noticed her mother hadn't even removed any of the fine jewels she'd come in. She'd kept them on like beautiful armour, though they looked ridiculous in the wooden *izba*. What's worse, Yaris' family must have thought so too, with their whispered words and furtive glances.

Sorona noticed Mara looking at her mother and understanding the child's thoughts said, in a strained voice, "Perhaps you would like to take your finery off, dear Zevena. We are but family here."

Mara's mother winced, but she obeyed. She took the heavy *kokoshnik* off and passed it to Mara, who was a little

puzzled as to what was expected of her. She looked to her grandmother for direction. Sorona Gontova said, "Take it upstairs to your father's room, child, and put it in the chest by his bed. And I know you're tired but come and sit with me for a while after."

Mara dashed upstairs, and when she returned, the room seemed less heavy somehow. Zevena still sat silent and straight, but without her *kokoshnik* she seemed smaller and not as cold. *Just different*, Mara thought, and the thought didn't please or displease her. It was as it was and no more.

Her cousins stared at Mara with open hostility, but she noticed with satisfaction there was also fear there now.

She sat herself back on the bench next to her grandmother, and drank warm fruity *kompot*, which, she was told by Sorona, was a special treat made just for this occasion. The other children had only a small cupful each and eyed Mara's big tumbler with envy.

The drink warmed Mara to the core and soon her eyes began to close. She didn't even notice when strong arms lifted her up and put her on a bed above the stove.

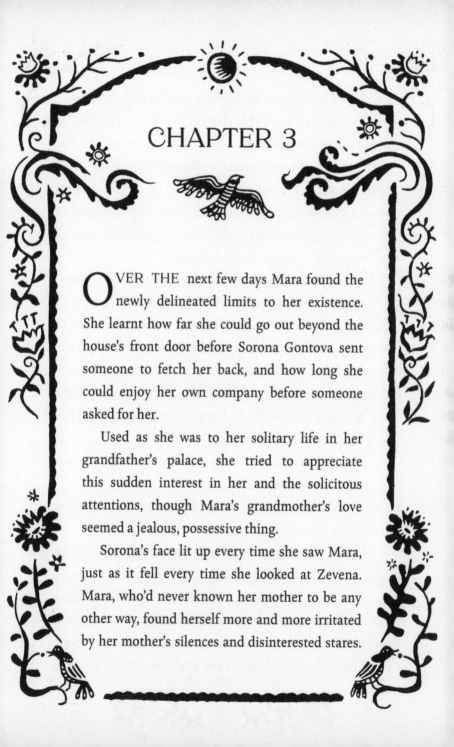

CHAPTER 3

OVER THE next few days Mara found the newly delineated limits to her existence. She learnt how far she could go out beyond the house's front door before Sorona Gontova sent someone to fetch her back, and how long she could enjoy her own company before someone asked for her.

Used as she was to her solitary life in her grandfather's palace, she tried to appreciate this sudden interest in her and the solicitous attentions, though Mara's grandmother's love seemed a jealous, possessive thing.

Sorona's face lit up every time she saw Mara, just as it fell every time she looked at Zevena. Mara, who'd never known her mother to be any other way, found herself more and more irritated by her mother's silences and disinterested stares.

She should make more of an effort or offer to help, instead of spending her days sitting straight in a chair or singing to herself outside the house.

Uncle Gnievos and Aunt Balinka made a valiant effort to befriend Zevena, but even they gave up after a week or two. Zevena would reply wordlessly when she could and in monosyllables when she couldn't, standing and staring until the buzzing of voices around her stopped.

The children made no efforts to befriend their new "aunt", or her child, for that matter. Mara didn't mind, though she blushed when she heard one of her young cousins whisper to the village children of the "ice spirits" when she thought she was out of Mara's earshot.

Every evening Zevena would tap Mara's shoulder and lead her onto the porch. And every evening she asked her daughter, "Do you need me still?"

Each time Mara looked her mother deep in her icy eyes and said, "I still need you."

Zevena would sigh and nod, and would go back to sitting in the chair farthest from the fire.

Litnev would come to the house most evenings, with the dark-eyed Torniv trailing behind, and the widower would spend hours with Yaris. Mara's father seemed better after those talks, which seemed to be the only reason Sorona suffered Torniv's presence. Sorona treated him more like a not-quite-domesticated dog than a boy, and Mara was told

not to encourage the boy's friendship.

Yet a child starved of love couldn't be expected to listen when a chance at companionship presented itself.

One evening, when the shadows lay low and long on the still-frozen earth, a few weeks after their arrival, Torniv didn't come in through the main door when his father did and instead scraped at the window shutters near where Mara always sat. She cast a glance in her grandmother's direction, but Sorona was in a deep conversation with Litnev. They both had their backs to Mara, and she felt a moment of anger that they would hide things from her, for they could have no topic of conversation except her father's declining health.

Mara put down her knitting and crept up to the window. She put her ear to the crack in the wooden panes. A stream of cold air tickled her skin.

Torniv's voice came from outside, "Can you get away? I want to show you something."

Mara glanced around. Zevena sat, as usual, in her chair and spun a white thread from black wool floss. The others in the room ignored her and her small miracles, though in the first days after their arrival they had all been awed by them. Yaris' brother was out working and Aunt Balinka was too busy to pay attention to her niece who now, quietly, snuck out the door.

Mara picked up her warm fur stole then put it down

again. Two days earlier, when she had wrapped it around her shoulders, her Aunt Balinka had opened her eyes so wide that her eyebrows had touched the tip of her colourful head scarf. She said nothing, but Mara understood. It was wrong for her, a mere child, to have such things. They were from *before*. The *now* demanded different rules.

So she picked up a patched-up woollen shawl and wrapped it round her shoulders before sneaking out.

"You took your time! Come on!" Torniv whispered furiously, barely leaving any gaps between his words. He ran ahead of her towards the woods and all Mara could do was follow.

"What is it you want to show me?" she asked. She winced as her boots squelched in the mud of the path separating the Gontov farmstead and the forest.

"You'll see!" Torniv flashed a smile and winked at Mara.

After a few brief moments, Torniv grunted with exasperation and grabbed Mara's hand. "You're *so* slow!" he said and began half-dragging her along.

"Wait, what's the hurry?" Mara laughed. She used her other hand to lift up the hem of her long skirt. If she came back covered in dirt, her grandmother would not be pleased. She would then be forced to explain who she went trudging through the woods with, and though Mara was a good-enough liar for an eleven-year-old, Sorona Gontova was nobody's fool. It was best to avoid any questions.

They came to a small clearing. Torniv put a finger to

his lips. "Shhhh. Look here."

On the ground, too weak to get up, was a little fawn; no bigger than a cat, and pure white.

Mara gasped, "What's happened to it? It's so small!" She crept up to the fawn and sat next to it. It rolled its eyes in horror so she didn't attempt to touch it.

Torniv had no such qualms. He crouched down next to the animal, dragging it onto his lap. He took a little clay jug out of his bag, pulling the cork out with his teeth.

"What is that?" Mara opened her eyes wide.

"I found her earlier this afternoon. I stole a bit from today's milking and mixed it with water. I don't know if the fawn will drink it but it's worth a shot."

"We should tell your father," Mara said. She reached out and touched the fawn's soft nose. The fawn flared its nostrils and she withdrew. "Or my Uncle Gnievos."

"You're that eager to see what she tastes like?" Torniv muttered through the cork in his teeth, and poured a bit of the white liquid into the fawn's mouth. The animal seemed confused for a moment but this lasted no more than a heartbeat before it began to lap up the milk.

"What?" Mara sat up straight.

"What else do you think our families are going to do with an abandoned fawn?"

"I didn't think about it." Mara said. She felt ashamed and startled at the thought.

Torniv chuckled, "Well, that's what I'm here for. Thinking for both of us."

She frowned and then shoved at his shoulder playfully. She still didn't much care for being teased, but she was getting used to Torniv's strange ways.

"So what are we going to do with it? We can't just take it to Sorona's house, and if we leave it here, it will die."

"She." Torniv said. "Not 'it'. She."

"Oh . . ." Mara smiled at the animal which now nuzzled into Torniv's warm belly.

"I kind of hoped you could tell me." He scratched his head under his tight-knitted hat. "Don't you have some magic trick you could do? With your grandfather being Stribog and all, could you do something?"

Mara crossed her arms. "A magic trick? Like what? You think I can magic up an ice barn? Or create a snow-doe to suckle her?"

He looked at her wide-eyed. "*Can* you?"

She couldn't help but laugh. "No, of course not!"

"Well . . . Then I guess I didn't think it through all that well. But we can't just leave her here."

Mara looked around. It would be dark soon and her grandmother would notice she was gone. She stood up and brushed away the bits of undergrowth which had stuck to her skirt. "We could call on Uncle Borovy? Or Aunt Borova?"

"Never heard of them," Torniv scratched his head.

"I don't think they're from our village."

She laughed and rolled her eyes. "No, I mean the forest guardian. The spirit of the forest," she elaborated, and smiled politely, waiting for Torniv to grasp her meaning. He looked at her blankly.

She shook her head and spread her arms wide. "A forest this wide and this healthy must have a spirit guarding it. That's Uncle Borovy's job. And he's always followed by young fawns." She nodded to herself and added, uncharitably, "Everybody knows that."

The fawn had fallen asleep in Torniv's lap and he shifted uncomfortably. "Everybody does *not* know that. I don't even know if you're crazy or silly or trying to trick me again." He seemed disappointed, like he had really expected Mara to pull a building or a magical animal out of her fingertips.

"I didn't trick you. You tricked yourself. I'm not crazy or silly. I thought Botrish people knew things like this," saying the last part under her breath but still Torniv's face darkened.

"At least I know *some* things. You're supposed to be a half-witch and you don't even have a little bit of magic in you. What's the point of that?"

"Witch?" Mara was startled.

"Oh, yeah ... Sorry, I didn't mean that ..." Torniv seemed a bit embarrassed. "Your cousins were all the way up and down the village bragging about living with an ice witch and it just stuck with me."

Mara's cheeks reddened.

"I know your ma's not a witch. I'm sorry I said that," Torniv said into his scarf.

Mara shrugged her shoulders like she didn't care. "I need to go soon. We have to ask Uncle Borovy for help. And the best way to find him is to call his wife. He always trails after her. Do you have any food on you?"

Torniv shook his head. Mara could see he was impressed, and she suppressed a smile and straightened her back. She liked knowing something he didn't, even if it was only how to call the simplest of the forest spirits.

"Any milk left in the jug?"

He held it to his chest, "It's for Sniezinka!"

Mara raised her eyebrows. "'Sniezinka?'"

He looked to the ground, suddenly embarrassed, "Only, she's so cute, with the white coat and all, she looks like a snowball."

"Fine." Mara reached out her hand. "Sniezinka needs more than the milk you brought her. She will need more in a couple of hours anyway. What will you do then? I need an offering."

Torniv handed over the jug, albeit reluctantly.

Mara stood up and looked around them. She picked up some pine cones and used Torniv's small knife to cut off one strand of her long hair.

"How do you know all of this?" Torniv asked. He tried to hide the amazement in his voice.

Mara smiled. "From the time I lived with my grandfather. He showed me how to call the spirits of the forest when he still thought I might be special. Anyway, these are old friends. Well," she hesitated, "I *say* friends, but don't get too comfortable." She placed the cones in a small circle on the ground and twisted the hair around them. Then she took the jug and poured the last few drops of milk between the pinecones.

They waited for a moment.

Nothing happened.

"Well, that was a waste of good milk!" Torniv said under his breath.

Mara shot him an annoyed look. "Just wait, will you?!"

A slow rumbling rolled over them, as the earth beneath their feet shook and shifted. The fawn woke up and squealed, trying to hide within Torniv's arms.

"Shh, don't worry, all's well," Torniv whispered, stroking the downy head, even though he was white as a sheet himself.

From under the pine cone circle, out of the ground, there rose a small figure. The pine cones fell around its head like a crown as it emerged. It lifted its head and two intelligent soot-black eyes took in the scene. The creature looked like an old woman, though her humanity was but thinly stretched over her bones. Her gnarled hands, wrapped around the top of a walking stick, had an extra joint, and her nose had a point which looked sharp enough to prick a finger.

"Hello, Stribog's granddaughter," the figure said.

"Hello, Aunt Borova," Mara smiled brightly. To Torniv's horror, the two embraced.

"Where's Uncle Borovy?" Mara asked. "We have something to talk over with him."

"Oh, you know," the old woman smiled and shook her head. "Always out and about, he is, playing tricks where he oughtn't. I can't bring myself to begrudge him, you see." She winked at Torniv who shrunk into himself, wondering what kind of mischief a magical creature might consider entertaining. "But I see you have made friends, Stribog's granddaughter? I didn't think you had friendship in you. Your mother and her sisters are cold things, but I suppose you have your father's warmth as well."

Torniv's mouth hung open but Mara was used to Aunt Borova's bluntness.

"I did make a friend, Aunt. And he found a new friend for Uncle Borovy," Mara said.

"Has he now?" A voice sounded between the trees.

Torniv whipped his head around, but Mara placed a calming hand on his shoulder. "Move slowly," she whispered and put her finger to her lips.

Aunt Borova laughed out loud as a flock of birds flew in and twirled around her. "You took your time, husband! What do you bring me?" she asked.

"Thaw on the air, and blood in the rushes," Uncle Borovy

said, as he emerged from between the trees. Mara dug her finger into Torniv's shoulder. He nodded though she could feel him shiver.

Uncle Borovy was tall, as tall as a bear standing on its hind legs. His skin had hardened into its folds, much like tree bark. His head was covered in leaves, and he wore a robe of moss. Rows of sharp teeth peeked from inside his mouth, and his hands were clawed. But most terrifying of all were his eyes, like drops of amber on his face, small and penetrating. He could bring blindness to those who displeased him with nothing more than those eyes. But Torniv definitely didn't need to know that, Mara decided.

"So is this the creature you seek to foist upon me, Stribog's granddaughter?" Uncle Borovy asked.

It took Torniv a moment to realise the creature meant him. "No, no!" he lifted up his hands. "She meant the fawn!" The silence which fell was a heavy thing and Torniv shrunk into himself.

"No," Uncle Borovy said after a while, his eyes swirling in their sockets. "It talks too much."

Mara laughed. Torniv tensed up and his hand flew up to cover his mouth. But then Uncle Borovy laughed too. Their laughter carried and warmed the air.

"I know what she meant, ungrown human," Uncle Borovy said. "I'd heard of this fawn. Its mother came to me after it was born. She smelled of blood and sickness. She could not care for it, for it came too early and too slow. For her baby, she asked for a quick death. But you feed it and ask for its life. Why?" He once more turned to Mara for an answer and this time Torniv knew to stay silent.

"It wants to live. And I promised to keep it alive," Mara replied.

"That is your promise, little one." replied the forest guardian, his head skewed to one side. "Nothing to do with old Borovy so far."

Torniv breathed a little easier. This he understood. This was a negotiation.

Mara frowned at Borovy. "Uncle, I'm surprised at you! With all the orphans you take in, what's one more?"

Aunt Borova crouched next to the fawn and stroked its head. She turned to Torniv and winked at him.

Uncle Borovy crossed his gnarly arms. "Who I look after is my business. It's not up to an ice urchin like yourself to tell me what I should do." His amber eyes swivelled, and Mara swallowed. Uncle Borovy liked children and his wife was fond of her, so she was safe. She was almost certain she was safe. But Torniv had no such guarantees. She had to be careful.

"I would never tell you what to do, Uncle Borovy. I'd

always believed your kindness and generosity to be near limitless. But I suppose we have found their limits at last. Such a shame, with the fawn so eager to live," said Mara while shaking her head. She sniffed and brought a sleeve to her eyes.

Torniv raised one eyebrow. Surely Uncle Borovy wouldn't be fooled?!

But the ancient creature rubbed its head, letting a shower of leaves and bark fall to the ground and grunted. "Well, now, that seems harsh, child."

Mara was now too invested in her performance to stop. She turned away dramatically and cupped her face in her hands.

"I . . . *sniff* . . . called you and Aunt Borova because I thought you the kindest of the forest lords . . . *sniff* . . . But don't worry, Uncle. . ." Mara said, wiping her eyes: the very picture of dashed hopes. "The spirit Perelesny told me he'd take care of it if I found your generosity lacking, so the fawn will be well. You don't have to worry about it." She glanced at Torniv, and he knew to keep quiet.

"Perelesny?" Uncle Borovy's head snapped back. His lips curled in a snarl. "What does that little nothing of a gnome have to do with my forest?"

Mara shrugged her shoulders. "He wanted to give you a chance to look after the fawn as a sign of respect, but he said he'd take it on if you were to 'miss your chance'."

"Indeed! And what would Perelesny want with a scrawny little fawn, too small to even sustain a wolfling?" Uncle Borovy narrowed his eyes. He spun around and walked right up to Torniv. He brought his head low enough so that Torniv could smell the moss growing in the cracks in his face. Torniv swallowed as he stared into Uncle Borovy's eyes.

"Is Stribog's granddaughter trying to trick me, little human?"

"Uncle, why would you doubt me when I have already said the fawn is not for you to concern yourself with—" Mara started.

"I want *him* to answer, child of the winds!" Borovy raised his voice. Mara closed her mouth and looked intently at Torniv. "Well, little human? What say you?"

Torniv looked at Mara desperately.

"Don't look to her for help, little one," Aunt Borova chuckled. "The winds always help themselves first."

"It's the truth," Torniv said. His heart was pounding and his tongue felt like lead in his mouth, but the only way was forward. "Perelesny took one look at the fawn here, and said she would be the strongest, proudest doe ever to walk these woods." Torniv's eyes twinkled and he smiled. Mara watched him in amazement. He was *good* at this. Torniv continued, "Perelesny will ride her under the moon and sleep curled against her warmth in Winter. He will feed her the sweetest berries and save her spring grasses for the snow days, and he will cherish and love her for all her days." This came out in a stream and Torniv sucked in a sharp breath when he finished, unable to look away from Uncle Borovy.

The creature stayed still for a while. Then he straightened his back and looked away from Torniv, once more addressing at Mara. "The fawn is mine."

Mara pouted. "You said you don't want her."

"DID I?!" Uncle Borovy roared. Aunt Borova wagged her finger at him and he calmed down, chastened. He cleared his throat. "Did I say such a thing? No, I did not! I had made no decision before, and now I have and I say I will have her."

"You won't love it like Perelesny will, I can see you won't," Mara said, her arms crossed, her eyebrows knitted together as she stared defiantly at the creature more than four times her size. "I can't give her away to be forgotten and starved when there are others who see her worth."

"I will prize her like the honey in my cup and like the moon's reflection in the lake. I will love her like the spring's first blossom and feed her from my own stores. She will feast on the milk of lynx and crunch the golden apples of the earthen orchards." There seemed to be something pleading in Borovy's voice now. "She will grow faster and stronger than any fawn that has ever stepped through these woods."

Mara was turned away from Borovy and only Torniv could see the small smile stretching her lips. She looked at Borovy over her shoulder. "And what of me?"

Borovy was taken aback. "What do you mean?"

Mara skewed her head to the side. "What will you give me for bringing you such a prize?"

Torniv cringed. She'd overdone it. She had pushed it too far and now the creature would get angry, and they'd be lucky to escape alive.

But Borovy said, "What would you have of me?"

Mara's face brightened. "You will let me ride it when its old enough, if I have need of it."

A silence fell over the forest and for a moment nothing stirred.

"Let it be so, child of the winds," Uncle Borovy said with a smile. "You have your grandfather's cunning about you, but your father's heart makes you care too much. You be careful of that heart, little one, because no cunning can save you from the pain it will bring you."

"What do you mean?" Mara said, but Uncle Borovy was gone already, a flurry of leaves twirling where he stood. The fawn was gone too, and Torniv was left staring at his empty hands.

"You've done well, Stribog's granddaughter. Your grandfather would be proud," Aunt Borova said with a chuckle. She hooked the end of her walking stick around Mara's neck and, without warning, pulled her head close. She planted a kiss on Mara's cheek. "I will see you sooner than you think, my love. Sooner than you think." Then Aunt

Borova simply sunk into the earth which closed above her head, leaving the pinecone crown lying in the dirt.

"That went better than I thought!" Mara said brightly. She turned to Torniv who was staring at his empty hands.

"Are you coming? My grandmother will be looking for me," Mara said.

Torniv wiped his eyes and sniffed. "I wish they had let me say goodbye."

"They never do," Mara said, and though her words were cold, the hand she held out to Torniv was warm.

CHAPTER 4

OVER THE next few weeks there wasn't a day without Mara sneaking out to spend time with Torniv in the woods. She introduced him to the small spirits of the forest and he showed her how to build a fire and hunt for rabbits with the sling he always carried tucked behind his belt.

"How come you never spend time with the other children in the village?" Mara asked one day as she watched Torniv push roasted potatoes out of the hot ash with a stick. He shot her a glance.

"Why do you think?" he said. He took out his little knife and blew on the potato as he sliced open its hardened grey skin. A cloud of steam rose in the cold air. It smelled delicious. Torniv used a piece of bark for a plate and passed a portion to Mara. "Sorry, I have no butter, but trust me, still good eating."

"An answer that's a question is no answer at all." Mara raised her eyebrows.

Torniv looked at his feet and stayed still for a moment. "Why don't your cousins invite *you* to play?"

"My mother," Mara answered without hesitation.

Torniv smacked his lips and leaned back, crossing his legs and turning his head to one side. "Same answer here. Nobody wants to be around the 'Botrish get', no matter how well-liked my father is. And in case anyone was likely to forget it, my looks are there to remind them I'm not one of them."

"But I look no different to my cousins," Mara said, biting her lip as she saw Torniv's hurt expression. She licked her finger and placed it on the hot potato to check if she could eat it. Her stomach rumbled, though her grandmother always ladled a grown man's portion of porridge into her granddaughter's bowl at breakfast. Mara knew it was a grown man's portion because she'd heard Aunt Balinka say it in jest.

"*You* may look no different, but your ma sits there every day, a reminder of who you are. The ice witch in your blood is just waiting to come out!" He raised his hands in mimicry of claws and made a snarly expression to emphasise his point.

"My mother is not a witch," Mara said. "She's the daughter of Stribog, who is a god."

"But what special blessing has she brought with her?"

Torniv spread his hands and shrugged as Mara gave no answer. "A few useful skills made my ma a witch in the eyes of the simple folk. A lot of useless magic makes yours one too. There is no arguing with things that are true." He dug into his potato, though it must have burned the skin on his fingertips.

"What happened to your mother?" Mara tested her potato again but it was still too hot. All the food she'd eaten since leaving the Stribog palace seemed too hot, so much so that she was always the last one leaving the table, blowing on her stew though all the others had finished theirs.

"My da says she died when I was little." Torniv used a piece of bark to scrape the inside of his potato skin. "I'm not so sure."

"Why not?" Mara opened her eyes wide.

"Well, for one," Torniv lifted one finger, "There's no grave. Not even a marker to which my father could point to and say 'Here, I lay her down'." He lifted the second finger. "Second, I heard some talk once in the market, some *babas* with their tongues wagging and too deaf to think others had ears good enough to hear them. They said my ma ran off, or was spirited away or something. Who knows?" He shrugged. "They say her kind never lingers. Why should I care for someone who cares nothing for me?"

"You'll find it hard to get anyone to care much for you, witch boy!" a familiar voice sounded between the trees.

Mara and Torniv stood up just in time to see three village children coming through the path. Mara noticed with a sinking feeling that the eldest of her own cousins was among them. He was the one who had ended up eating the maggots he'd intended for Mara, and the nasty glint in his eye told Mara as clear as anything that he hadn't forgotten.

"What do you want?" Torniv said, but his tensed shoulders and wide stance told Mara this was not the first time he had had to face this.

"My cousin shouldn't be out here alone," the boy smiled nastily. He was about a year older than Mara and nearly a head taller so she had to raise her chin to face him. "*Especially* with a Botrish pup." He turned his head to face Torniv and grinned. "My *babcha* will be very disappointed to hear of this."

The other two kids, a red-headed girl and a fat boy Mara recognised from the market spread out to the sides, surrounding them.

Mara stepped in front of Torniv and folded her arms. "I bet she'd be more disappointed to hear of you threatening us."

Her cousin feigned shock, his hand flying to his chest. "Threaten? I'm so sad you'd think that! And here, we came all this way to save you, after hearing you cry in the forest – after *he* attacked you!" He pointed at Torniv.

Mara was confused. "I wasn't crying!"

Her cousin smiled. "Oh, but you will."

He grabbed Mara and turned her around, holding her arms behind her back, twisted painfully. On his signal, his two friends launched themselves at Torniv.

The two peasant children were both older and bigger than Torniv but he moved fast on his feet, punching, scratching and biting. There was nothing fair about the fight, and though Torniv didn't pull any punches, in the end, he was one young boy faced with opponents who were accustomed to playing dirty and determined to do harm.

"No! Don't!" Mara screamed at the two children as they kicked and punched Torniv, who lay in a ball on the ground, protecting his head. Mara wriggled and tried to kick at her cousin, but he held her tight, laughing.

Then she stopped. She looked up and closed her eyes. A whisper escaped her lips.

"By the blood and the thorn, and the breeze and the storm," she muttered, and let her head hang limp, swaying gently from side to side.

The two pummelling Torniv stopped and looked up. The red-haired girl pushed some dirty hair out of her face. "What's she saying?" Her eyes went wide and Mara smiled at the fear woven unmistakably through the village child's voice.

"Stop it, witch!" Her cousin pulled her arms higher up behind her back. The pain in her shoulders seemed unbearable but she just kept chanting.

"The wind will come and the wind will go. Grandfather!" She opened her eyes and looked up. "Bring the Winter storm to those who'd attack your kin! Bring cold and misery to their lives and frost to their families' orchards! Freeze the air in their lungs till they're drowned in their own blood!"

The two children who'd attacked Torniv took a step back. The fat boy looked up, fearfully. "The witch is doing it! Look! The wind! It's picking up!"

The nastiest smile Mara could muster stretched her lips. "You attack a child of the gods, stupid, you will reap your reward!"

Her cousin let go of her arms. "Stop it, Mara! Call it back!"

She laughed. "And why should I? Perhaps I will leave you three frozen and dead in the forest for the wolves to find you!" She turned around and flashed her teeth at her cousin. "You should have thought twice before messing with the gods, little human!" She pushed her chest forward and threw her arms in the air.

"I'm sorry! I'm sorry!" Her cousin cowered in front of her. He cast a look towards his two friends but they were already gone. "Please don't kill me!"

Mara looking at him in contempt. "You will never again bother my friend Torniv. You will never touch him again!"

"Yes, yes, I promise," the boy covered his head, his eyes streaming.

Mara dropped her arms. "Then you may live. For now."

She sniffed. "You'd better go and change your breeches though."

Her cousin didn't have to be told twice. He shot like an arrow through the forest, leaving Torniv and Mara alone in the clearing.

Once he was gone, Mara ran up to Torniv. "Are you ok?"

Torniv struggled to his feet, wiping his bloodied nose with his sleeve. "What was that?"

"What was what?" Mara was so relieved to see that Torniv was alright, she didn't immediately understand him.

"I thought you had no powers!"

"Oh, that!" Mara laughed. "I don't."

"But . . ." Torniv looked up. A bruise was already forming on his cheek. "There was the wind in the trees . . ."

Mara chuckled. "Has it stopped?"

"Umm, no."

"This is Prissan, Torniv," Mara said, taking his hand. "There's always wind here."

CHAPTER 5

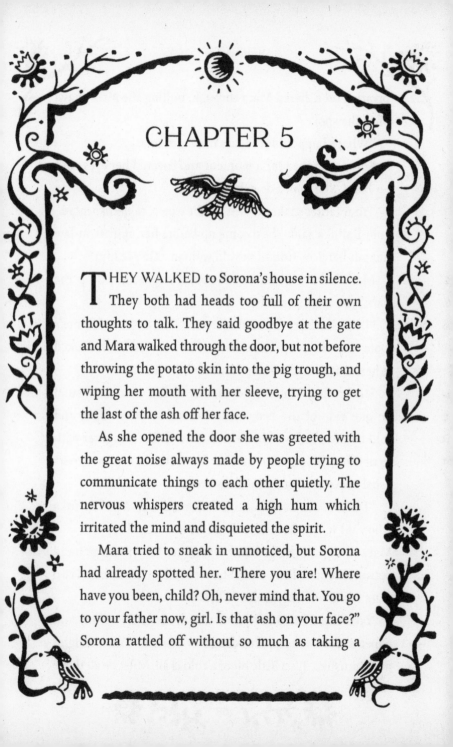

THEY WALKED to Sorona's house in silence. They both had heads too full of their own thoughts to talk. They said goodbye at the gate and Mara walked through the door, but not before throwing the potato skin into the pig trough, and wiping her mouth with her sleeve, trying to get the last of the ash off her face.

As she opened the door she was greeted with the great noise always made by people trying to communicate things to each other quietly. The nervous whispers created a high hum which irritated the mind and disquieted the spirit.

Mara tried to sneak in unnoticed, but Sorona had already spotted her. "There you are! Where have you been, child? Oh, never mind that. You go to your father now, girl. Is that ash on your face?" Sorona rattled off without so much as taking a breath, and ushered Mara through, pulling the girl's shawl off as she spoke.

"What's happening?" Mara managed to ask.

Sorona stopped for a moment and covered her eyes with her hand. She took a deep breath.

"Your father's taken a turn for the worse, *slonechko moye*." Aunt Balinka said. She'd come up before her mother-in-law and put her arm around the old woman. "Go see him."

Mara blanched. She spun around and bounded up the stairs, two steps at a time.

"Da?" She burst through the door. The air in her father's room was thick with the stench of sweat. Her father looked at her, as if he had trouble focusing his eyes.

His brother, Uncle Gnievos, was sitting on a small stool on one side of the bed, while Zevena stood straight and cold by the window. She turned towards her daughter with something like pity crossing her face before it returned to its usual expression of polite disinterest.

"Da? *Babcha* Sorona said, I mean, it was Aunt Balinka who said it, but *babcha* looked like she would cry and . . ." Mara ran up to the bed and placed her father's large hand between her two little ones. She screwed up her face and two tears ran down her cheeks. "Oh, Da . . ."

Yaris lifted his other hand with some visible effort and wiped a tear away from his daughter's cheek. "That's alright, my Marushka. It's a little bit of a cold is all. Must be all those years in the ice palace catching up with me." He caught his brother's expression and added, "Just a little joke, *moya zabka*. Nothing to do with Stribog. I'm human and humans get ill sometimes. And sometimes . . . I'm sorry, *Marushka*, but sometimes we just don't get better . . ." He said the last in a whisper.

"Don't say that, Yaris!" Uncle Gnievos shook his head and cast a glance at Mara. "Don't scare the little one. *Mamusha* has sent off for the medicine woman. She's the best one we've ever had in the village, and she healed the pig farmer's leg last winter, though it had turned black as soot already and felt no cold nor heat, or so he says. And then there was the midwife two years back, with a cough stained with blood, and they say—"

Yaris cut off his brother with a movement of his hand. "No, Gnievos. No lies for my little one. No wise woman will help me. Isn't that right, my love?" He turned to Zevena.

Mara looked at her mother, whose face might have appeared immobile to strangers, though Mara could see the slight twitch of eyebrow and the slight tensing of the jaw. Zevena nodded.

Yaris reached out for Mara. "Come here, *Marushka*." He pulled her closer to him and embraced her. "It won't be long, *moya zabka*. I'm sorry."

"Can't you do something? Anything?" Gnievos said to Zevena. He spread his arms wide. "All your magic can't

make whatever illness this is crawl out of my brother's chest?"

Zevena shook her head. "I'm but the lesser of my father's children. I could bring frostbite and turn your fingers dead and black. I could freeze your chest till the shards of your own shattered lungs choked you. But I can't help Yaris. We are not built to heal." She paused for a moment, searching for the right words. "I'm sorry."

"I don't care if you're sorry," Mara heard herself say. She turned her tear-stained face towards her mother. "What's the point of being Stribog's daughter? What's the point of all this . . . this show-off magic, if you can't even save him?"

"*Marushka*, don't . . ." Yaris whispered, but Mara was too angry to stop now.

"What's the point of *you*?!" She pointed her finger at Zevena who stood still as a statue. "What good are you if you can't save him?"

"I'm just myself, daughter of mine," Zevena said quietly. "I never claimed to be any good to anyone." With that, she turned around and left the room.

"So this is what you left us for?" Uncle Gnievos said. His voice came out like a growl. "An icicle of a wife, whose magic is only good for looking pretty and spinning white cloth?"

"She made me no promises, she's broken no vows." Yaris shook his head and smiled, "She was enough for me."

"This *isn't* enough." Mara turned her face towards her

father's chest and cried, her sobs shaking her whole frame, while Uncle Gnievos sat close by, his face in his hands.

The evening light brought Sorona upstairs to her son's room. She brought a plate of stew she didn't expect Yaris to eat and a cup of bone-broth she was determined to make him drink. Uncle Gnievos had already gone downstairs and it was just Mara and her father in the room. Mara looked up as the door swung open, angry at the intrusion.

"I brought you this, *synek*, you need your strength," Sorona said with a strained smile. She sat on Yaris' bed, rather than the stool, and straightened his covers.

Sorona noticed her granddaughter and stroked her cheek affectionately. "*Marushka*, shouldn't you be with your mother? Let your da rest, girl,"

"No, *mamusha*, I will rest soon enough. I want her here," said Yaris.

Sorona took in a sharp breath and focused on smoothing the invisible creases on the covers. "It's bad talk, *synek*. You'll get better. You'll see. You'll feel better, as soon as you drink this broth. I've cooked the bones and herbs for hours and there is nothing like that for bringing blood back to your cheeks."

Yaris smiled as the severe Sorona Gontova prattled on.

Sorona Gontova never prattled, of course, and so he drank the broth, taking quick, tired breaths between each sip, and he pretended to try the stew, and he kissed his mother's hand as she stroked his cheek.

"Now, you'll rest. You'll get better. All will be good once more, *synek*." Sorona turned her face away from her son and hobbled towards the door. "Come, *zabka*," she said to Mara. "You need to eat too."

"Go with her, *Marushka*," Yaris whispered to Mara. "Your *babcha* needs you." He tucked a stray lock behind her ear. "You can come back after you've eaten."

Mara bit her lip and folded her arms like she used to do when she was younger. But her father kissed her forehead and her grandmother sniffed like she was choking back tears and there was nothing to do but join her.

Mara walked behind her grandmother, as Sorona grunted her way down the steep stairs. The *izba* was unnaturally quiet. The soup on the stove gave off a pleasing, metallic smell and Aunt Balinka was embroidering something in the corner, every now and again stroking the hair of one of her children, who all liked to congregate at her feet, as she was always full of good stories and even songs on occasion. But her mouth was silent that evening and, one by one, the children at her feet dozed off.

Zevena sat in her usual spot, ignoring the occasional dark look from Uncle Gnievos.

Mara ate her dinner and listened to Sorona talk about the spring markets and the sow's piglets and the quality of woollen floss and all the other little things her grandmother thought could erase the sad knowledge between them.

But, at long last, when her grandmother was all out of reasons to keep her, Mara crept upstairs to her father's room. She crawled under the covers and made herself small, placing her head on his arm. She listened to his raspy breath and traced a pattern on his palm with her finger until she too was asleep.

Mara was woken by a low keening, which rose into a scream more frightening than any *upior*'s. Strong hands grabbed Mara by the shoulders and pulled her out, still half-asleep, from under the covers and whisked her away so the bed disappeared from her view.

Mara rubbed her eyes and peered, disoriented, at the face of her Uncle Gnievos, who held her so tight she could barely breathe. "Don't look, girl, don't look," he said to her, quickly, the words running in a fast stream towards her uncomprehending ears. Mara was confused. Who was he speaking to? Where did he not want her to look? Why was Babcha Sorona screaming, why was—? *Oh*...

Mara wriggled out of her uncle's grasp and shot up to

the bed. For a moment she thought they must've all been mistaken. Her father was asleep. Sorona's broth had helped, it had chased away the sickness and all was well.

Except it wasn't.

Zevena, who'd been standing in absolute silence, approached her daughter and put her hand on Mara's shoulder. "Tonight I won't ask if you still need me," she whispered into her daughter's ear, and she held her, as she'd never done before, while Mara cried.

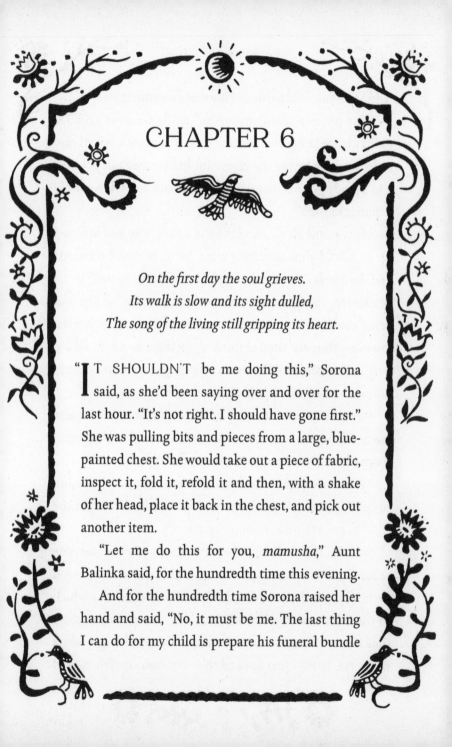

CHAPTER 6

On the first day the soul grieves.
Its walk is slow and its sight dulled,
The song of the living still gripping its heart.

"IT SHOULDN'T be me doing this," Sorona said, as she'd been saying over and over for the last hour. "It's not right. I should have gone first." She was pulling bits and pieces from a large, blue-painted chest. She would take out a piece of fabric, inspect it, fold it, refold it and then, with a shake of her head, place it back in the chest, and pick out another item.

"Let me do this for you, *mamusha*," Aunt Balinka said, for the hundredth time this evening.

And for the hundredth time Sorona raised her hand and said, "No, it must be me. The last thing I can do for my child is prepare his funeral bundle

and I will not fail in this as I have in everything else."

"You haven't failed, *mamusha*," Uncle Gnievos said. He cast a glance at Zevena, making it clear to anyone who'd care to look where he lay the blame for his brother's death. "He was already gone by the time he came back to us. It was only a matter of time."

Mara heard all this and yet she didn't. She was scooped up in Aunt Balinka's strong arms, being rocked backwards and forwards like a baby, and she allowed herself to be comforted, though she wasn't yet quite sure what she was being comforted for. Her da, it was something about her da, but every time she tried to think about it her mind would fog over and all she could do was cry, though she didn't exactly know what she was crying about.

Her aunt was murmuring some words which didn't quite reach Mara, though the monotonous sound of her voice soothed her. One word kept coming through though.

"What's *Navia*?" Mara suddenly looked up at her aunt, so quickly she startled the good woman, who'd thought the child in her arms was half-asleep already.

Aunt Balinka looked at the rest of the family but everyone seemed too occupied to pay attention. She paused and chewed on her lip a little, as adults do when asked questions which to them have answers so obvious and so well-understood, they needn't be answered. Like *why is the sky blue* and *why is water wet*. Things just are and they are their own thing and to let your mind settle on them threatened to unravel the certainties of life one depended on.

"Navia is . . ." Aunt Balinka thought for a moment and rummaged through her internal stores of legends and stories. She began rocking again, readying herself for the storytelling. "Navia is where we all go when we leave this world, for the Root Soul in us lasts for always, but our bodies do not . . ." She cast a glance at Zevena and hesitated, "Most of us anyway."

"The Root Soul?" Mara perked up.

"The immortal, everlasting part of us, sweetling." Balinka brushed a strand of hair off Mara's earnest face. "We each have two souls within us, entwined for as long as we live. Once our bodies die, our twin souls journey westward for forty days to Navia, the realm of Veles, deep within the sea waters. Once they arrive, the human soul rests up in the stars and the Root Soul goes to roost in Veeray, Perun's tree of life, till it's ready to come down and live once more."

"So da is in Navia now?" Mara perked up.

Balinka shifted uncomfortably under the intent stare of the child's light brown eyes. "Not quite yet. It takes forty days for the soul to travel there."

"So we can still stop him?!" Mara said breathlessly. She raised herself up and cupped her aunt's puzzled face between her two small hands. The hopeful smile on her face dimmed as Aunt Balinka shook her head.

"No, *slonechko*, no human can bring another's soul back." She caught the eyes of Uncle Gnievos and stood up, urging Mara to sit back down. "I'll be back. Rest now. I will bring you something warm to eat, you haven't had anything all day." Aunt Balinka wouldn't have liked to admit it, but she was relieved to have a task of some substance to attend to, and to no longer sit under Mara's intense stare.

But I'm not all human . . . Mara thought to herself, and the little part of her that was ice and wind rejoiced.

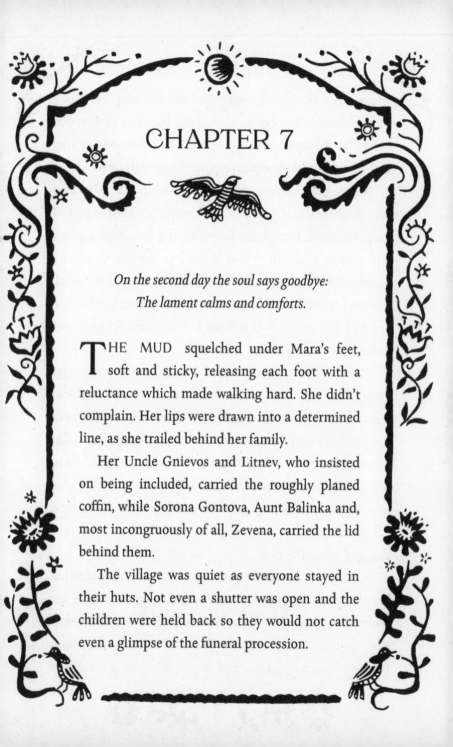

CHAPTER 7

On the second day the soul says goodbye:
The lament calms and comforts.

THE MUD squelched under Mara's feet, soft and sticky, releasing each foot with a reluctance which made walking hard. She didn't complain. Her lips were drawn into a determined line, as she trailed behind her family.

Her Uncle Gnievos and Litnev, who insisted on being included, carried the roughly planed coffin, while Sorona Gontova, Aunt Balinka and, most incongruously of all, Zevena, carried the lid behind them.

The village was quiet as everyone stayed in their huts. Not even a shutter was open and the children were held back so they would not catch even a glimpse of the funeral procession.

Sorona wailed loudly while Balinka chanted. The noise startled Mara at first, but now it had just become a background noise, like the squelching of her boots, and the crows cawing in the field in complete contempt of the ragged scarecrows.

Her mother had put on her white fur coat and her fine *kokoshnik* for the occasion. Mara thought her mother looked quite beautiful, though the jewels on the *kokoshnik* seemed duller than when they first arrived at Sorona Gontova's house, and the bottom of her fine coat trailed in the mud. Zevena looked fine, of course. Just not the same kind of fine as when her beauty was reflected in the ice mirrors of her father's palaces.

Mara looked at her mother's silver hair, which no longer seemed the silver of ice, but more the white of a week-old snow, melting among the dry grass. She caught a glimpse of her mother's bare forearm as the sleeve fell away when her mother raised the coffin's lid to her shoulder. Zevena's skin was still pale blue, but it was no longer the sparkling blue of a sky seen through ice. It was now the colour of a lack. An absence of sun, an absence of life. The blue of a corpse dragged out of the river.

And what was it on her arm? Mara squinted, not trusting her own eyes. Yes, goosebumps were marking the skin on her mother's forearm. Not from the cold, that'd be impossible. But then anything but the diamond-smooth, diamond-brilliant Zevena had seemed impossible just a couple of months before. As she diminished in the eyes of those around her, she seemed to diminish in her own self as well. Yet Mara wondered if the change was all in Zevena, or if she herself had changed, so that her mother seemed different to her now?

They reached the burial place, where Uncle Gnievos had already dug a hole that morning.

The ground was dark, like it was everywhere around the village. The good black soil which made every grain of wheat grow tall and golden, so Sorona had told Mara.

She shuddered.

The hole that would swallow up her father's coffin was like a dark gaping mouth, moist and hungry.

The men put the coffin down on the cold ground, on top of the lengths of rope that would serve to lower it into the hole.

Sorona fell to her knees beside the coffin, and with shaking hands placed some dry flowers on Yaris' chest. His body had been washed by his mother's hand, in defiance of tradition. She wouldn't let anyone else touch him. She placed a little knotted kerchief, filled with herbs, by his head and bent her own, letting her tears fall onto him.

"Ah, *synek*, why have you left me? What for? My bones

are rotting within my flesh, and your bones were strong and still you left me." Sorona caressed Yaris' cold cheek and muttered, as if to herself, though Mara heard the beginning of a melody build in her grandmother's throat.

This was the beginning of the *lament*, as her aunt had explained earlier. The song of grief, unprepared, unplanned, coming as a chant from the depths of the soul and allowing the dead to leave with the knowledge that, however short their time, it was well spent, for they were loved.

Mara listened to Sorona Gontova, who sang in a raspy voice, sing of her pain and her grief and her loneliness. Mara wiped her tears with her sleeve. *Forty days.* Forty days within which she could reverse her grandmother's pain.

She longed to tell them all that she would not let it be the end, but Mara was Stribog's granddaughter, and she knew when to hold her tongue.

As Sorona sang, Uncle Gnievos and Torniv's father placed the lid onto the coffin and lowered Yaris' body into the grave.

Sorona finished her song and, wiping her face with her scarf, turned to Zevena. "Now it's your turn. You, who were a wife to him, or ..." she hesitated, "... close enough to a wife as makes no difference. Sing for him."

Zevena cocked her head to the side and watched Sorona with her ageless eyes. She nodded. "Very well."

Zevena raised her arms and the wind stilled, though they were out in the open. The quiet was sharp like the cold and

Mara realised they'd all been holding their breaths.

Then Zevena sang.

There were no words. Music poured forth, enveloping them all. A living thing, made of a cold, distant beauty. Mara closed her eyes. It was beautiful and all-encompassing and so very, very wrong.

Sorona felt it too, and she set her lips in a line, though her chin trembled still. "Is that all you have for my son?" she demanded when Zevena finished.

Mara's mother looked at the old woman in surprise.

Sorona leaned on her stick and shook with a seething fury. "Where's the feeling? Where's the heart of you? Where are the words to send my son on his way? Where is the song of your grief, the song of your love?"

Zevena looked at Sorona for a long time. In the end, she simply said, "My father Stribog is the God of Winter Winds and God of Music, the God of Air, and of Silver too, but he is not the God of Poetry."

"And are you so wholly ruled by his limits?" Sorona spat, "What's the point of *you,* then, even though you're so beautiful?"

The rest of those assembled watched this exchange. Some, like Aunt Balinka and Litnev, with discomfort, and some, like Uncle Gnievos, with a quiet anger, which Mara suspected more than equalled his mother's.

Aunt Balinka put her arms around Mara, who, though

she appreciated the gesture, couldn't bear to be touched. She stepped forward, a silent child among the squabbling adults, and picked up a handful of the black wet soil. She whispered a promise into it and threw it on top of her father's coffin, before turning from them and walking away.

Zevena noticed, and with little care for Sorona's continued outburst, she rushed to her daughter.

They walked without touching, without words.

Once Mara decided nobody would be able to hear them, she stopped, and turned her small face towards her mother.

"I don't need you anymore, mother."

Zevena stared at her for a moment, her expression inscrutable.

Mara thought maybe her mother didn't hear. "I said I don't—"

"I know what you said," Zevena said. "I'm trying to decide if your words are true or whether they just sound true. Your father would have known, but I cannot tell."

The wind rose and picked up Zevena's twin braids so that they flew about her face.

"Ah . . ." she said and smiled.

And Mara knew then that there was a permission on the wind, an invitation to return. But her mother stood still and her daughter would remember and be grateful for that small pause for all the days of her life.

"I will ask you again, and you will tell me the truth.

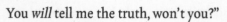

You *will* tell me the truth, won't you?"

Mara nodded.

Zevena took a breath and asked, "Do you still need me?"

Mara sniffed, clasped her small hands together, so tight they turned white. She took a deep breath.

And then she lied.

Zevena smiled, and suddenly she was as beautiful as before, as beautiful as she must have been on that day, many years ago, when Yaris first saw her in the woods. Zevena lifted one of her braids, and with her nail, as sharp as the sharpest knife, she cut it just under her chin. She placed the braid, long and silver, and soft as a baby's breath, into her daughter's hands.

And then Zevena Stribogovna was gone, nothing but the wind blowing through the spot where she stood a moment ago.

The child she left behind wrapped the braid around her neck like a scarf and walked back towards her grandmother's house.

She had to hurry. Her father wouldn't wait and she had to leave before the morning.

Mara sat through the funeral feast, her eyes down, replying only when addressed by the multitude of neighbours

and well-wishers who rolled through her grandmother's house. They came to commemorate Yaris, as well as eat the specially prepared food, which so soon after winter was an extravagance few could afford.

Sorona Gontova was the picture of strength, her dignified expression once more covering up the sorrow.

Nobody mentioned Zevena's absence, though Mara knew she'd be asked about it soon enough, as well as about her mother's silver braid, still wrapped around her neck. Aunt Balinka sat close to Mara and urged her children to also sit next to her, a show of support Mara didn't need, though she appreciated the sentiment behind it.

All Mara thought about was the pack of food and spare clothing waiting for her in the barn. Her fur cloak was by the door, and she'd be gone before the sunrise.

Torniv stood by his father and watched Mara with his dark eyes from a distance.

Mara would have told him then, but for the people around her. Instead, she kept her eyes down, and her face still, and her voice low lest it betray her.

At long last the people left. Litnev was the last to go, and he seemed so diminished and so low, his son held his father's hand as if he were still a baby. Mara smiled. It was kind.

"We will clean tomorrow," Sorona said. "I'm tired now. Balinka?" She turned to her daughter-in-law. "I would appreciate it if you'd let the little ones share my bed over the stove tonight." She turned to Mara. "And you too, *Marushka*. My bones feel brittle and my skin feels cold tonight, and I know yours does too. It's a comfort to have my grandchildren around. Together it all feels less real, and at night an old heart can't cope with reality." She turned towards the stove and took off her headscarf and the pins holding her hair. It fell down to her waist, surprising in its length and thickness. The grey waves dwarfed her.

Aunt Balinka's younger children squealed at the prospect of sleeping on top of the stove, where it was warm and comfortable. They all raced to take off their outer clothes and boots and climbed up.

Sorona gave Mara half a smile. "Don't let their high spirits upset you, *moya zabka*. They didn't grow up knowing your father and so they don't grieve for him like we do. But it's good for our grief to be softened by their joy." Sorona gave Mara a kiss on the forehead and, slowly, with Uncle Gnievos' help, she climbed into her bed.

Aunt Balinka finished cleaning and went to bed, but not before giving Mara a tearful hug.

Uncle Gnievos lingered for a moment. "Your father was a good man. And your ma, well, she's gone now. But we're your family, you know." The big man shifted uncomfortably and swept his hair off his wide forehead. "You're not alone here, *Marushka*. We have five children now, for we count you among them. And you will lead a good life here, you'll see."

Judging he'd said enough, he gave a curt nod and followed his wife up to their room.

Mara crawled into the bed above the stove, cramped with the little children and her grandmother. There were elbows and feet everywhere, as Sorona's grandchildren all tried to find a comfortable space, and the heat coming off their little bodies made the area unbearably hot. But Mara stayed very still, and closed her eyes, and quietened her breathing, until there was nothing but sleep and calm all around her.

As quietly as she could, she crawled out of the bed and snuck to the door. Not daring to wrestle with her clothes there, she threw them over her shoulder, picked up her boots, and crept out of the house. The door hinges were well oiled and didn't make a sound.

Once outside, Mara breathed in the cold, brisk air with pleasure. "There once was a girl and the girl was me," she muttered to herself. The words gave her courage. In the story, the grief and the fear became a part of the adventure. She quickly pulled on her wide trousers, and her knee-length dress tied with a wide belt. The most practical clothes she owned, though they too were decorated with silver thread. She tucked the hem of her trousers into her boots and snuck to the barn, where she'd left her pack of food and spare clothes.

First she gave a handful of oats to her father's pony. It was too old to go with her, and would likely be dead before she

returned but it nuzzled its nose under her arm and whinnied a goodbye. Mara kissed the horse's forehead and wiped away a tear. There was no time for that. No time to be sad. She crouched down and rummaged through the hay. A breath caught in her throat.

The pack she had prepared wasn't there!

Again and again she buried her arm elbow-deep in the hay and again and again it came back empty. It was there, she was sure of it. She had left it one step away from the trough, and to the right of the threshing tools. Her heartbeat sped up. What if her grandmother woke up? She'd notice Mara wasn't there. And she couldn't go back to the house to get more food, they'd hear her!

She froze as she heard a voice behind her.

"Are you looking for this?"

CHAPTER 8

In the night the soul can still pretend,
Not seen and not heard,
A cat's soft paw on the soft grass
Moving through the world, already forgetting
A face and a voice.

"Torniv!" Mara's jaw dropped. "What are you doing here? How did you find my things?" She reached out to take them but Torniv held the pack away from her. He wasn't smiling.

"And why do you need a pack of food and spare clothes? And a knife as well?" He raised the small knife Mara had stolen from her grandmother's kitchen. She tried to snatch it, but he quickly hid it behind his back.

Mara's hands balled into fists. She took a deep breath and relaxed. "Give it back, Torniv."

"You're leaving, aren't you?" Torniv narrowed

his eyes. "I knew it! I knew it as soon as I saw you at the feast! What are you planning? Are you going back to your grandfather's palace?" Torniv stomped his foot, all the pent-up frustration pouring out of him. "Never mind that nobody there wants you or waits for you! Never mind you have a grandmother, one who loves you and braids your hair, and sings to you – I heard! And an uncle and an aunt who care for you and feed you, and cousins, and . . . and . . . never mind your friend, who has nobody here to talk to him or treat him like he's somebody, and . . ." Tears were running down Torniv's face now. He wiped them away angrily with his sleeve. "All *you* care about is your fine clothes and fine foods and I don't know what—"

"No, Torniv, you have it all wrong!" Mara managed to say.

Torniv sniffed, suddenly embarrassed. "So . . . you're not leaving?"

"Well . . ." Mara hesitated. "Not exactly. I have to go, but I'll return. I need to bring my da back."

Torniv looked at her as if she was mad. "Your da's dead . . . Mara . . . You know he's dead?"

Mara tightened her lips into a line. "Forty days," she said.

"What?"

"Forty days to reach Navia. Forty days in which I can get him back."

"You can't," Torniv said. "Everybody knows you can't. No human can enter Navia alive, and no human can bring back the dead."

"Aha!" Mara said, lifting her finger. "You see it's like the old riddles. A thing is the way it is unless you find a way for it to not be. No *human* can enter Navia. No *human* can bring back the dead. And what am I?"

Torniv shifted uncertainly. "You're human. Like me."

"My grandfather is the God of Winter Winds, Torniv! I'm Stribog's granddaughter and I'm going to bring my da back!"

"Ok," said Torniv after a while. His dark eyes were very serious all of a sudden. "I'm coming with you."

"No."

"I wasn't asking."

"You're not like me! It could be dangerous!"

"You'll need me then."

Mara tried a different tack, "What about your father? He'll be worried sick."

"What about your grandmother?" Torniv was back to his usual self now. He crossed his arms and stood firm. "Won't Sorona Gontova fret and worry for her favourite grandchild?"

"That's different! I'll come back with her son!"

"And I will come back with my father's best friend."

Mara hesitated. "And if you don't come back?"

Torniv stood in silence for a moment. The air came out as steam as he breathed out. "Then they will say Torniv turned out to be his mother's child after all."

Mara tried objecting more, but Torniv made it clear he would rather wake the entire village than let her go alone.

They set off together and walked quickly past the sleeping houses, crossing the muddy path and the field. Mara turned towards the forest.

"See, you'd already be lost without me," Torniv said. "Navia is West. You're going in the opposite direction."

"Do you know how fast a soul travels?" Mara asked without turning around.

"No . . ."

Mara turned to him with a smile. "We'll be needing a steed."

The forest was dark. Mara walked sure-footedly, but Torniv tripped over the roots and the stones till he protested and demanded that Mara let him light a torch.

Mara waited impatiently, pacing the ground, as Torniv looked for the wood and moss and then struggled to light it.

"You're making me nervous, Mara. It won't take too long."

"It's the second night. The second of forty nights. Or is it forty days only?" Mara bit her lip to stop it from shaking. Her fingers ran along the silver braid wrapped around her neck. "After that, my da's souls will split into two and then I don't know how I'll get him back!"

"We'll get there faster if we're not eaten by wolves and if I don't crack my head open on the way. There!" Torniv lifted the lit torch triumphantly.

Mara gave no sign she had heard him. "I think we're far enough from the village." She knelt down in the dirt and pulled out a morsel of bread from her bag. She couldn't see farther than her hand so she just drew a circle in the dirt with her finger and sprinkled the crumbs inside.

She waited for a moment. "Aunt Borova. Uncle Borovy. I'm here and I'm here for you. Please come out." There was silence. Tears filled Mara's eyes. "Please."

"Since you asked so nicely," Aunt Borova's voice came, as if from the ground itself and there she was, sure enough, rising from the soil. Her expression was stern, though her eyes twinkled in the light of the torch. Though she wore no crown, there was a circle of light around her head, as if the hasty drawing Mara had made in the sand took on a form of its own.

"Thank you for coming, Aunt Borova," Mara said respectfully.

"Yes, never mind that," Aunt Borova said. "You best be on your way before my husband comes. He's mighty displeased with you, for the trick you played on him."

Torniv's eyes widened in terror, but Mara kept a straight face. "A trick, Aunt?"

Aunt Borova chuckled and shook her head. "You're Stribog's and no mistake. My husband went to Perelesny straight after you foisted that early-born fawn on him, to gloat, of course. And wouldn't you know? That was the first time Perelesny had heard of it." She wagged her finger at Mara. "Borovy was mighty upset about it all. Tricksters dislike being tricked, you know."

"And the fawn?" Mara asked.

Aunt Borova poked her with her long finger. "Well and better than well, as you know or ought to know. Borovy keeps his promises and he promised to love that fawn dearly and love it he will, though he does resent you for forcing this love upon him."

A change in the air alerted them all to a different presence.

"I did tell you to leave, child!" Aunt Borova said.

Torniv grabbed Mara's arm.

Mara stood firm though, straight and motionless. And there Torniv saw it, how she could look so like Zevena that the very air around her stilled.

"You can't outrun the forest, Torniv," she whispered.

CHAPTER 9

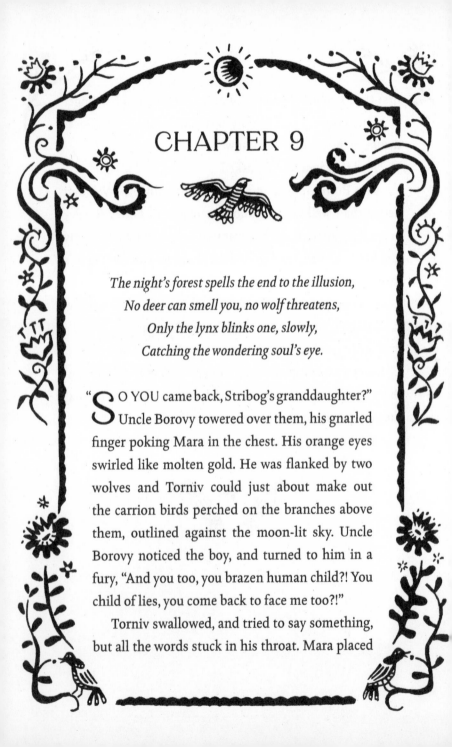

The night's forest spells the end to the illusion,
No deer can smell you, no wolf threatens,
Only the lynx blinks one, slowly,
Catching the wondering soul's eye.

"SO YOU came back, Stribog's granddaughter?" Uncle Borovy towered over them, his gnarled finger poking Mara in the chest. His orange eyes swirled like molten gold. He was flanked by two wolves and Torniv could just about make out the carrion birds perched on the branches above them, outlined against the moon-lit sky. Uncle Borovy noticed the boy, and turned to him in a fury, "And you too, you brazen human child?! You child of lies, you come back to face me too?!"

Torniv swallowed, and tried to say something, but all the words stuck in his throat. Mara placed her small hand on his shoulder and it calmed him.

"Why wouldn't we come back, Uncle? Where else can we go in need, but to our friends?"

Uncle Borovy stared at her for a moment, and Torniv saw the fury quieten in the forest god's eyes, replaced by something like amusement. The giant laughed then, a sound that shook the needles from the tall pines. "You come seeking favours, child of winds? When I should twist your neck off your shoulders and feed you to my wolves, you have the nerve to ask for favours?" He laughed again.

"I brought you a friend last time I was here, dear uncle, and, like we discussed, I come looking for my reward," Mara said, unperturbed.

Torniv chewed on his lip. It was all ridiculous. She barely reached Borovy's knees. And yet she faced him squarely as if she was his equal, as if his wolves weren't circling around them.

"A friend is it? That scrawny little fawn, close to death, and deserving of it too, for being weak and useless. Foisted on me through trickery?"

"And yet you love her," Mara said.

Uncle Borovy lowered his body to face her. He bent his back and his knees and crouched in front of them. The bark-like skin covering his flesh creaked as he did so. His flaming eyes were so close to Mara's face that she could feel the heat coming off them.

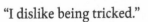
"I dislike being tricked."

"Still, you love her."

Uncle Borovy was very still. He nodded his head. "I love her."

Mara nodded. "Then you're welcome. And now I come to take her off your hands."

The forest guardian opened his mouth, then closed it again, staring at Mara.

"I need to leave, and I need to leave now, and I have need of a mount, fast and sure footed," she said with a curt nod.

"She's not grown," Uncle Borovy said in a whisper.

"I need to ride her," Mara said.

"You can't have her."

"You promised me, Uncle." Mara pointed a finger at the forest guardian. "You know as well as I you can't keep her."

Uncle Borovy struck his fist on the ground by Mara's feet.

"You can't ride her! She's much too small!"

"That is for me to decide." Mara stood very still, her arms crossed on her chest, as if the waves of a god's fury weren't shaking the very ground she stood on.

"You can't have her, for I love her and I will not be parted from her!"

Mara smiled. "What will you give me for her then?"

Aunt Borova, who kept quiet through it all burst out laughing. "She's got you there, husband!"

Uncle Borovy turned his anger on his wife, "You be silent!"

"A near-human girl-child, no more than eleven years of age, and she tricked you!" Aunt Borova was holding her stomach, bent double with the enjoyment of her husband's predicament. She wiped a tear from the corner of her eye. "Remind me never to bargain with you, little one! Your grandfather would be proud."

Mara didn't smile. She stared at Uncle Borovy, unblinking. "I need to ride something. I need to travel fast if I'm to reach Navia before my father."

Aunt Borova stopped laughing. Her husband just stared, something like pity crossing his eyes. "You can't be serious, child," he said, "The dead don't come back."

"My da will." Mara set her lips into a line.

"No," Uncle Borovy said. "You will die on that road and I will not let any of mine die with you, just because you see fit to throw your life away."

"You made a promise," said Mara.

"I know what I owe you, wind-creature." Uncle Borovy scratched his head, causing a flurry of leaves to fall to the ground. "I might have a solution."

He pointed a gnarly finger at Torniv. "He will be your mount."

"Me?" Torniv's face turned white. "I'm not a horse!"

"Nor a deer, nor a wolf, nor a bear, nor a fox. Nothing half as useful." Uncle Borovy smiled. "But you *could* be, if you want to help the little trickster here, of course."

Mara turned to Torniv, her eyes down. "You don't have to . . ."

But Torniv, who was just about to refuse, heard himself say, "I do."

Then Uncle Borovy raised his hand, and the forest grew quiet. Not a chirrup nor a breath could be heard. And then, something almost like a whistle, a quiet susurration at first, and growing louder. A whirlwind surrounded them, and on Uncle Borovy's outstretched palm, hair by hair, a cloth appeared, growing, till it spilled from his hand. Fur, silky and rich brown, appeared on the cloth. It grew till a whole bear skin was hanging off the forest god's arm.

"Wear this skin, boy, and you will turn into a bear. Take it off and you will become human again."

Torniv approached slowly. He reached out and let his fingers touch the soft fur. It seemed no more than a skin, a dead thing, hung on the walls or placed on the floors of the rich *boyars*.

Uncle Borovy leaned down. "I can see the hunger in you, little human. Be very careful where the hunger leads you, for if you keep the skin on for longer than two days and two nights, then by sunrise on the third morning you will no longer control your transformation. Instead you will forever be a bear by day, and a human by night, and no magic of the winds or human hand will be able change that."

"I'll do it," Torniv said. "I want it."

"Are you sure?" Mara whispered. She'd never seen her friend like this. There was a hunger in his eyes which she didn't recognise.

He nodded. "I want it." He reached to take the skin, but Uncle Borovy snatched it away, a mischievous twinkle dancing in his amber eyes.

"Ah, but this is more than a mount, child of the winds, and I owe you no more than a mount. This is old magic, and it's true and real, and worth something more, I think." He turned to Mara with a smile.

"What do you want?"

"That silver braid around your neck. Give it to me and you will have the skin."

"No!" she said, her hands raised to her neck.

"Maybe not the *entire* braid," Aunt Borova chimed in suddenly, startling Mara. "Enough to wrap around your wrist once. You can keep the rest."

Torniv placed his hand on Mara's shoulder. "Give it to them. It's not that much. The braid is so long, you will still have most of it left. Not a high price to get your father back."

Mara hesitated. Uncle Borovy nodded and started to turn away.

"Wait!" Mara called after him. "I'll give it to you!"

Aunt Borova had hobbled over almost before the words had left Mara's mouth, and she grasped the silver braid. She wrapped it once around Mara's wrist and with one long

sharp nail she severed the measure of hair from the rest. It glittered in her hands as she turned to her husband. "Give them the skin," she said and, not waiting for him to respond, she sank into the earth.

"Here you go, boy," Uncle Borovy handed the bear skin to Torniv. "May it be of some good to you." And with that he disappeared.

Mara and Torniv stood in silence for a moment. Mara tied the end of the cut braid in a loop around her neck, then she looked at their long-extinguished torch and the trees around them. "Look," she said. "It's almost dawn already."

"Then we had better be on our way," Torniv said. He lifted the heavy bear skin and threw it over his shoulders.

And then he screamed.

CHAPTER 10

On the third day the soul looks to the water.
Missing thirst and hunger it will never feel,
It relishes the memories of sustenance,
And quenches the longing in its breast.

MARA LOOKED on in horror as the magical bear skin enveloped Torniv.

There was a sickening crunch as his bones cracked and grew and fused together till he filled the entire skin. He rolled and writhed in pain on the cold ground He pulled his head back and let out a deafening roar. He then sat on the ground panting, no longer a human boy, but a large bear instead, towering over Mara.

"Torniv?" Mara said in a whisper.

Torniv-the-bear pricked his ears and turned his dark eyes towards Mara, blinking.

He opened his mouth and the voice which came from his throat was like a growl, though it formed human words: "It's me."

Mara wanted to thank him, to say how grateful she was for what he'd done. But she just looked into his eyes and said, "I think we'd better go."

Torniv nodded and lowered his hulking frame till she could climb up onto his back. She grabbed handfuls of his fur for safety. Once he was sure Mara was secure, he rose and turned West.

"We must avoid the roads and villages," he said. "It might take a while longer. Your da's soul can travel in a straight line."

"Then you'd better run quick," Mara said.

Torniv nodded. He stretched his paws and bounded towards the horizon.

Mara yelped at first at the shock of the movement, but she soon got used to the wave-like rhythm of the bear's pace.

"You're fast!" Mara said with a laugh.

"I'm not yet! Just getting the hang of this!" Torniv replied and sped up.

The pines went by them in a purple-brown blur as the hours passed and the morning turned to noon.

They stopped for lunch in a meadow, where a fallen tree made for a comfortable seat for Mara.

"Do you want to take your bear skin off so you can eat?" she asked.

Torniv-the-bear shook his huge head. "If it hurts as much to take the skin off as it does to put it on, then I'll wait, thanks." His shoulder muscles rippled and dipped in what Mara assumed was a shrug.

"Well, just remember what Uncle Borovy said. You don't want to get stuck like this."

Torniv yawned in response. He rose and turned to the forest.

"Where are you going?"

"To eat. I'm a bear so I assume I can eat bear things."

"Don't go crazy!" Mara called after him. "You'll fill up on grass and acorns and the human you will have a bellyache once you take the skin off."

Torniv didn't reply, so Mara turned to her lunch. After a whole morning of riding, her whole body was sore, and her hands were cramping from holding on to Torniv's fur.

Her stomach growled. She carefully unwrapped one of the small parcels she'd packed. It contained cheese and a large cabbage-filled *pierog* from the funeral feast. She uncorked the clay jug with *kvass* and drank in big thirsty gulps.

She felt a moment's guilt that she didn't have enough to feed Torniv, but then she didn't even have enough for herself if the trip was to take nearly forty days. Anyway, he could get food as a bear. This made her feel a bit better, but she saved a bit of *kvass* for him in any case.

She raised her hand against the sun and watched the pink

light as it shone through the thin parts of her skin, lighting up the small veins. Her hand seemed human. There was nothing of Zevena's diamond brilliance about it. Nothing of Stribog's changeable, fluid, shape-shifting magic. Mara sighed. If her hand was so human, what about the rest of her? Was her heart just human? Was her mind? Perhaps she was "of the winds" in name only and upon reaching Navia she'd find just how powerless she really was.

She thought about what Aunt Balinka had told her about the human soul. How it split in two on entering Navia: the mortal, human part seeking rest, and the immortal Root Soul travelling up the Veeray tree to be reborn. Mara wondered if her souls were human too, or if, in death, at last her grandfather would lay a claim to her.

She lay down on the fallen log and turned her face towards the sun. Spring was a cold business in the forests of Prissan, but Summer was already on its way. Mara could feel it in her bones.

Summer had been a strange time back when she had lived in her grandfather's palace. It was always Winter there, and her grandfather would stay home more than usual, teeming with pent-up energy and blowing through the halls, invisible till he chose to make himself otherwise.

When she was very small, and there was still hope of her godly lineage manifesting itself, her grandfather would sometimes take her with him on his travels. He'd lift her up

and speed through the woods, frosting the grass as he went. He didn't talk much, and wasn't much interested in what she had to say, so she'd just enjoy the speed of the wingless flight.

She stretched her arms above her head and closed her eyes. The warmth of the sun was soothing, though she didn't need its heat as others did.

She hummed to herself as she waited for Torniv. She was eager to be on her way, and yet her muscles needed rest. The humming helped to ease the tightness in her chest, which squeezed the very breath out of her whenever she thought of the passing hours which took her father closer and closer to Navia. Three days gone since he died, that left thirty-seven, she calculated in her head. She hoped it would be long enough.

"That's a lovely braid you have there, little bird!" A cheerful voice roused her. "Not yours, that is, thin and sad brown as it is, but the sparkling silver one around your neck, little bird! Heidash likes that, oh yes he does!"

Mara sat up straight and looked to where the voice was coming from.

A dark figure hovered between the trees. It had legs and a head like a mountain goat, with large horns curling on the sides of its ears. Its eyes shone like torches, and Mara could just make out a smile, with teeth large enough to grind bones.

"Oh yes, Heidash likes it very much . . ."

"Go away!" Mara screamed.

"You tell Heidash 'go away', but Heidash wants to stay, little bird." The creature came out into the light. As he did, Mara noticed the garlands of spring flowers wrapped around his horns, and the beautifully carved stick he leaned on. In the light, Heidash looked far less frightening than she'd first thought, though his teeth were still sharp and his claws were still long. *Rusalki* didn't look frightening either, until you were stupid enough to get close.

"How about a trade, little bird? You give Heidash that shiny, sparkly, silky, shimmering silver thing around your neck and Heidash will give you a garland of flowers, never-wilting."

Mara began backing away from the creature. It walked towards her slowly, balancing oddly on legs not designed for a two-legged gait.

"I won't give you a thing! Stay away!" she shouted. She wanted to sound threatening and confident, but her voice came out as a high-pitched squeak instead.

"Here." Heidash smiled, which only made him look more terrifying. He took one of the garlands off his horn and held it out in his clawed hands. "Pretty flowers, for some pretty hair. Not even all of it, just most of it. Little birds like pretty flowers. And these won't wilt in your hand nor shrivel on the

vine, oh no, these will always be pretty, long after the flesh falls off the little bird's bones, the flowers will still be pretty on the earth that covers them."

"I don't want your stupid flowers!" Mara tightened her fists. "It's my mother's hair, and I won't give it to you!"

Heidash seemed taken aback. He cast a furtive look around. "Your mother? With the silver hair? Heidash didn't know, Heidash didn't see. The little bird doesn't look like Stribog's kin, and only Stribog's kin has such pretty hair." Heidash cast a sly look at Mara, who took a step back.

The creature chuckled to himself. "But Stribog's far away. There is no frost on the grass and no snow in the meadow. The little bird is very far from The House of Winds. Won't the little bird talk with Heidash? Maybe trade with Heidash?"

Mara opened her mouth when a brown blur rammed into the creature. Torniv-the-bear had returned and now he stood up on his hind legs and roared. Heidash cowered.

"Heidash is sorry! Heidash would never hurt the little bird who's friends with the big bear!" Heidash covered his head with his clawed hands and grovelled at Torniv's feet.

Torniv exchanged a look with Mara. She shook her head. "He crept up on me when you were gone."

Torniv lowered himself to the ground, though it didn't stop Heidash from writhing on the ground like an eel out of water. "Did it threaten you? What sort of a creature is it?"

At that Heidash raised his head. "Just Heidash, dear bear-creature. Just the old Heidash, meeting your friend on his walk. The little bird hummed so pretty, Heidash came to listen. Heidash likes pretty songs, and the pretty little bird hums a pretty tune."

"I've never been called pretty," Mara said. Now she was safe, she looked at the strange creature with a mixture of disgust and sympathy. "Tell me, why do you want my mother's braid?"

Heidash smiled hopefully. "The little bird will give Heidash the pretty braid?"

"No."

"Oh." His face fell, in as much as Mara could tell. He did have the head of a goat, after all.

"Why did you want it?" Mara asked again. Heidash begun to draw circles in the sand with one claw. He put his bottom lip out, like a small child denied a treat.

"Answer her," Torniv growled.

"The pretty braid is of Stribog's kin. It protects from fire, protects from frost. Protects those who are lost." Heidash sniffed loudly. "Heidash is often lost."

Mara's face turned white.

"Mara . . ." Torniv said. "When Uncle Borovy asked for a measure of the braid . . ."

"I didn't know what I was giving away," Mara finished. She placed her hand over her eyes. *So stupid.* She should

have known better, she should have asked. Uncle Borovy had paid her back alright.

"You gave Uncle Borovy some of it already. Do you think it will weaken its powers?" Torniv asked.

"How would I know?" Mara said, nervously biting her nail. "I didn't even know it was anything more than a gift from my mother, something to remember her by."

Torniv growled as Heidash tried to crawl away while they talked. "Where do you think you're going?" Torniv said. He lowered his large head close to Heidash's and bared his fangs.

Heidash rolled onto his back and raised his clawed hands up. "You don't need the old Heidash. Heidash will be on his way if the kind bear-creature lets him go."

When Torniv didn't move away, Heidash sighed and turned to Mara. "Braid isn't whole? That is not a problem for the little bird. Well, maybe a little problem but not a big problem – like no braid at all would be. The little bird should look after the pretty, pretty, very pretty braid now..." Heidash paused, his longing gaze on the hair round Mara's neck. "And if the little bird shared the braid already, she could share a bit more with Heidash?" He gave a wide smile.

"Don't count on it," Mara said.

"Oh..." Heidash sighed. "But now will you let Heidash go? Heidash is no trouble. No trouble at all to the little girl and her bear-friend."

"You can go . . ." Mara said with a sweet smile. Heidash breathed out with relief and began to stand up. Torniv, who understood Mara's meaning perfectly, however, placed a heavy paw on the creature's chest. Heidash squealed. Mara continued, ". . . as soon as you tell us how to get to Navia."

"The little bird wants to go to Navia?" Heidash said.

"You heard her," Torniv said.

"The easy way or the hard way?"

"There's an easy way?" Mara asked.

"Of course!" Heidash beamed at her. "The little bird can just . . . die. Then the little bird would go to Navia and then she would give Heidash the pretty, pretty ha—" Torniv's paw squeezed the air out of Heidash.

"And the hard way?" Mara asked. Torniv lifted up his paw slightly.

"No need for the bear-creature to be so hard on poor Heidash. Poor, poor Heidash told the little bird what she wanted to know . . ." Heidash turned on his stomach and covered his head.

"Heidash, focus," Mara said.

"The hard way is the far way, the long way, the dangerous way. The little bird may die. If she dies out there, Heidash won't get the pretty braid and then nobody has it. Waste, waste." Heidash spread his fingers so he could peek between them with his beady eyes. "The little bird must fly to the sea. By the sea the little bird must find a boat to sail West.

Ten days. Ten days of sailing the little bird must do. And there will be pretty things on the sea. Pretty things and hard things and hungry things too. But maybe the little girl doesn't die. Then the little girl gets to see Baba Latingorka. Then the little girl will die for sure, for certain, for as definite as the honey's sweet. Then little girl will go to Navia. But if the little girl is a very lucky clever thing, and defeats Baba Latingorka, then the little girl can go to Navia also."

"That's not much to go on," Torniv said.

Mara looked at Heidash and something like pity stirred in her chest.

"Let him go," she said.

"He might know more."

Mara shook her head. "I doubt he'd tell us. Go, Heidash."

Heidash jumped onto his goat legs and backed away, with an eye on Torniv. "The little bird is kind and sweet. Heidash will give one last tip to the sweet bird: You'll be hungry, but don't eat, if you Veles want to meet. There be milk and bread in cave, milk and bread will fill your grave."

With that Heidash disappeared.

"We'd better get going. The day won't last much longer, and it's a long way to the sea," Torniv said.

"Thank you . . ." Mara said with a shudder. "For earlier. For rescuing me. If I were on my own . . ."

"Well, you're not," Torniv said, suddenly embarrassed. "Now hop on."

"Wait," Mara said. She bent down and picked up a flower, which must have dropped off Heidash's garland. She smiled and breathed in deep. "I'm ready."

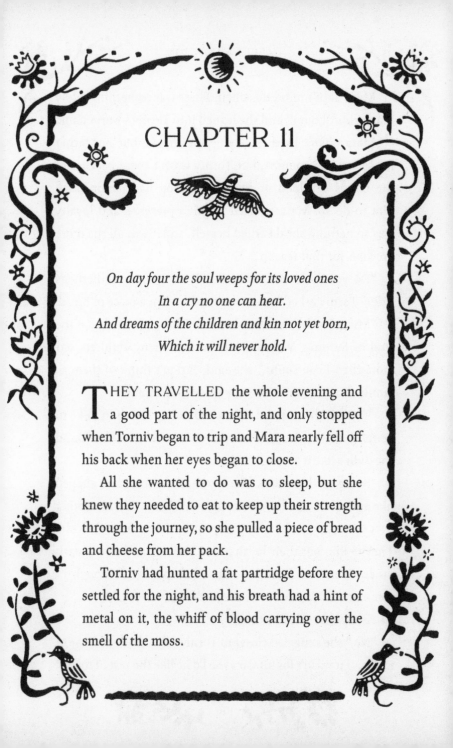

CHAPTER 11

On day four the soul weeps for its loved ones
In a cry no one can hear.
And dreams of the children and kin not yet born,
Which it will never hold.

THEY TRAVELLED the whole evening and a good part of the night, and only stopped when Torniv began to trip and Mara nearly fell off his back when her eyes began to close.

All she wanted to do was to sleep, but she knew they needed to eat to keep up their strength through the journey, so she pulled a piece of bread and cheese from her pack.

Torniv had hunted a fat partridge before they settled for the night, and his breath had a hint of metal on it, the whiff of blood carrying over the smell of the moss.

Mara didn't mind the smell. There was something oddly reassuring about it, and she leaned into Torniv's warm flank.

Mara wasn't used to relying on anyone but her father for safety and comfort, but Torniv wasn't there because of the bonds of blood or because Stribog had commanded him to do so. Mara realised Torniv's presence and loyalty was something she'd earned herself, and it was all the more precious for that reason.

"Do you have any other family on your grandfather's side?" Torniv asked her, as she crunched on a piece of bread.

"My grandfather has a brother I have never met – the God of Summer Winds, Dogoda. And many children. Far more than I can count," she said. "I don't think of them as family though. Not in the way you'd understand."

"Try me," he grunted. Mara had noticed he didn't like to be reminded of the differences between them. She'd found she didn't like it so much either.

"Some of them look like my mother, some are shaped like animals, some have no form at all, just a breeze turning over your cup and laughing as your lips chap from the cold. They're kin, but their loyalty is to Stribog, and not to each other. Even that is only because he's powerful enough to command it. Winds have little in the way of love."

"But you're not like that."

"No," she snuggled closer to Torniv. "But that's because of my da. If it wasn't for him, maybe I'd be like the rest of them."

Torniv sniffed at her and curled his large body around her. "You wouldn't be," he said with absolute certainty, as they both drifted off to sleep.

All the next day and night they travelled again, though Torniv had to take his bear skin off before the sun dawned on the third morning of his being a bear.

The transformation was painful, and resulted in a moment's embarrassment for them both when they realised the magic of the bear skin did not conveniently retrieve Torniv's clothes from Mara's bag and onto his back. Mara stood with her back to Torniv as he dressed.

"Huh," he said, wiggling his toes inside his straw *bast* shoes.

"What?"

"It feels strange to be on two legs." He leaned forward and back, rocking on the balls of his feet. "I guess we'd better get going. We won't be as fast as before, and your da's soul needs no rest."

"Can you hear that?" Mara suddenly stopped. Torniv looked around. The slightest breeze ruffled the young pale leaves on the aspens. The air smelled sweet with the moss and the wet earth. The sounds of the forest barely imposed on the calm.

"I can't hear anything," Torniv said. He suddenly looked worried. "Do you think Heidash is following us?"

Mara shook her head. "He couldn't wait to get away. Besides he would have pounced the moment you took off the bear skin if he had. This is ... different ..." She stood on tiptoes as if that could make her peer farther into the forest.

Torniv visibly relaxed. He readjusted the pack on his back and turned West again. "It's just the forest. Come, we'd better keep going."

Mara hesitated but she followed Torniv, nonetheless.

Another hundred paces or so, and she stopped again. She grabbed Torniv's arm. "Listen!" They stood still for a moment. Mara's eyes were round like the moon when she said, "Can you hear it? It's like music, it's—"

Torniv's face turned pale. "I can hear it now."

"What do we do? Do we hide?" Mara shivered, though there was no wind.

"Why would you hide from me, honey child?" A voice soft and high came from between the trees. Torniv's shoulders relaxed, even as Mara spun around in terror.

"Who are you?! Show yourself!"

"I'm here. I'm just as impatient to meet you as you are to meet me."

Mara gasped as the most beautiful woman she'd ever seen emerged between the aspens. She was tall, with sun-kissed skin, and long black hair, which she wore loose, so it fell down to her knees. Her eyes were large and had a kindly expression, and her arms were outstretched, like she was offering them both a hug.

Torniv had a glazed expression, and a silly little smile curled up the edges of his mouth.

"I'm Kania, honey-child. And you are . . ." the woman said and turned her head this way and that like a curious bird.

"We're uninterested," Mara said. She tried to be brave, and stood with her feet wide apart, planted firmly into the ground. "Be on your way and we will be on ours." She tried to pull on Torniv's arm, but he stood still, like his feet had grown roots. "Torniv, come on . . ." she whispered.

"You are lost, my children, and I always find those who are lost."

"We are *not* lost!" Mara said. She meant to sound confident but, even to her own ears, the words sounded petulant and weak.

"Oh, I think you are, inscrutable creature," Kania smiled at her. "And *you*, you are not quite what you seem, I think." The woman hummed under her nose and Mara felt as if a fog had risen in front of her. She touched her mother's braid by her neck and she could see clearly once again.

The woman frowned slightly but then turned to Torniv with a smile. "What about you, my handsome boy? You've been lost for a while now, I believe. And now you've found me."

"I found you . . ." Torniv repeated.

"You have missed me, haven't you, my boy?" Kania opened her arms. "Motherless for so long, when I've been here all this time. I've been waiting for you."

"Ma . . ." Torniv took a step forward.

"No!" Mara grabbed his arm. "Torniv, that's not your mother!"

"Nasty girl, so jealous," Kania said with a frown. "So jealous of my sweet boy." Her face was still as she looked long and deep into Torniv's eyes. "Come to your mother, darling. I've missed you so. It's been so long . . ."

Torniv shook Mara off. Tears were streaming down his face.

"*Mamusha* . . . You left me! Why did you leave? They said you were dead!"

"I'm not, my love. And I will never, ever leave you again." Kania stood, beautiful and still, though the wind had picked up, kicking up the leaves so they twirled around her feet.

"Torniv, she's tricking you, can't you see?!" Mara tried to grab Torniv again, but he looked at her with vacant eyes, his face contorted in sudden and unrecognisable anger.

"You let me be! You have your mother! So what if she's cold and silent—she's beautiful and a goddess! I have a mother now too! And she's special and she's beautiful! You don't want me to be happy!"

Mara stood back, as if slapped. "That's not true! You know that!"

But Torniv had already turned towards Kania. With one leap he was with her, his arms wrapped around her waist. Kania placed her elegant long-fingered hand on his head and stroked his hair. "That's right, my boy. You're with *mamusha* now. And I love you. And I will never leave."

The long folds of Kania's dress fluttered like a sail, and behind her, two wings rose up, grey and featherless, like a bat's. The woman locked eyes with Mara and smiled as a whirlwind enveloped her and Torniv.

Mara gasped as Kania and Torniv's feet left the ground. Without another thought, Mara jumped.

She grabbed Torniv's leg and pulled.

"Are you joining us, little girl?" Kania said. Mara felt her body being pulled upwards.

Mara wrapped both her legs and arms around Torniv's leg and her fingers searched out her braid. She closed her eyes tight and whispered "A braid of Stribog's kin. 'Protects from fire, protects from frost, protects those who are lost.'"

A gust of cold wind broke like a wave over Kania's whirlwind. The winged woman screamed, a terrifying, inhuman sound, which shook Torniv out of his stupor.

He looked up at Kania's face, contorted with fury, the beauty fading away fast, as Stribog's winds battered at her disguise, revealing the sharp teeth and the owl-like eyes. Torniv screamed and struggled against the creature's grasp, with Mara still holding onto his leg.

Kania pulled him closer.

Then she let out a yelp of pain and Mara and Torniv tumbled to the ground.

After a moment, Mara and Torniv looked around them, dazed.

The creature was gone and, once more, there was no wind blowing through the woods.

"What did you do to her?" Mara asked, rubbing her face.

Torniv slowly blinked then faced her. "I bit her," he said with a shrug.

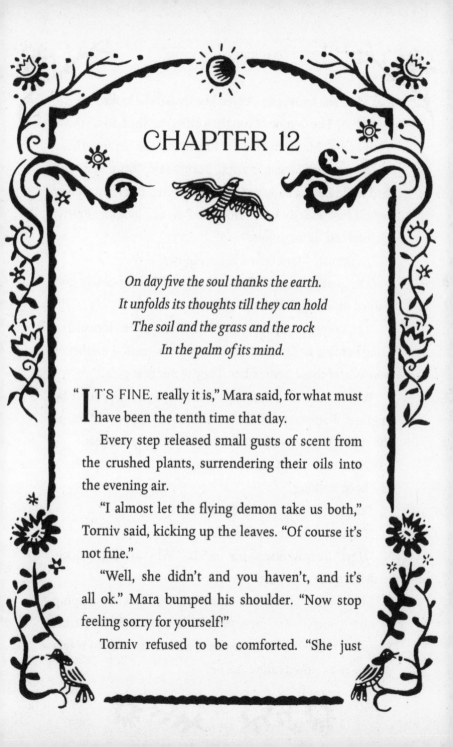

CHAPTER 12

On day five the soul thanks the earth.
It unfolds its thoughts till they can hold
The soil and the grass and the rock
In the palm of its mind.

"IT'S FINE. really it is," Mara said, for what must have been the tenth time that day.

Every step released small gusts of scent from the crushed plants, surrendering their oils into the evening air.

"I almost let the flying demon take us both," Torniv said, kicking up the leaves. "Of course it's not fine."

"Well, she didn't and you haven't, and it's all ok." Mara bumped his shoulder. "Now stop feeling sorry for yourself!"

Torniv refused to be comforted. "She just

looked ... You know, I don't even know what she looked like ..."

"Who? The demon? I caught a glimpse. She had all these teeth and—" Mara wiggled her fingers next to her mouth.

"No, not *her*. I mean my ma," Torniv said. "My da said she died when I was a baby so I never knew her. But Kania made herself look exactly how I imagined my ma looking. Pretty. Magical. All those things."

"Magical?" Mara raised her eyebrows.

"Oh, just forget it!" Torniv hunched his shoulders and walked onwards, facing the ground.

"I can't forget it, you just said it." Mara leaned forward to bring her face under Torniv's. "You want a magical mother? I have one of those, remember. They're not that great."

Torniv snorted. "Your ma's hair saved the day, don't be ungrateful. Anyway ..." He reached out to support Mara, as she stumbled over a root. "Are you ok? We need to rest."

"No, I'm fine," Mara waved away his offer of help. "Let's just keep walking."

"You need rest. Let's sit down."

"I'm fine!" she snapped back.

"Hey!" Torniv raised his hands. "Why are you prickly with me all of a sudden?"

Mara bit her lip. He was right. She shouldn't be snapping at him. "Sorry," she managed. "What you said. It's true. I need rest but I know my da is well on his way to Navia and we're as slow as slow can be."

"Don't worry," Torniv picked up the pack and slung it over his shoulders. "Tonight, I'll put the skin back on and you will feel the wind in your hair again." He shot her a smile and she almost felt comforted.

"Do you think we're far from the sea?" She tried to look ahead into what seemed like a never-ending forest, stretching out in front of them.

"I don't know," he said as they walked. "As a bear I could smell the brine, but then . . . I was a bear and could smell a great many things, some from very far away. I haven't had much experience of being a bear, so I don't know how to judge the distance." He shrugged his shoulders.

"You make a very good bear." Mara managed a smile.

"Oh yeah?" He seemed pleased by her compliment.

"Yeah, maybe your ma had a bit of witch in her after all." He beamed. "Or a bit of bear . . ." she added with a mischievous smile.

"If only!" He laughed and kicked up a bit of the soil.

They walked and ran for five more days and nights, resting when they could, and eating whatever Torniv-the-bear managed to find in the forest. On the morning of the eleventh day after Yaris died, the trees grew sparser until they gave way to grass, growing in dry clumps along a beach.

The air smelled like seaweed and fish. Mara breathed in deep. In the past and for his own amusement, her grandfather had brought her the scents of all the places he

visited. She'd smelled the rich, cloying smell of the roses which Stribog had frosted over too early. She'd known the scents of soured milk and a fat goose cooking over the fire. She'd even smelled the sea. But to see it was another thing altogether. To see it was to instantly feel small.

"Navia is somewhere over there . . ." she said. Torniv saw her fidgeting hands and placed his over them in a gesture both familiar and comforting.

"We'll get there in time."

Mara turned to face him. Her dark-circled eyes were wide with fear. "How?" she demanded. "How are we going to cross . . ." she waved her hand vaguely in the direction of the sea, ". . . this?!"

She sat in the sand and rested her chin on her fists. "How far do you reckon we can see from here? A mile? Ten? More? Do you see Navia?"

"Nope," Torniv sat down next to her.

Mara put her face in her hands. "We'll never get there in time!"

"Not if we keep sitting here, we won't," he said.

She turned her eyes towards him.

Torniv shifted uncomfortably under her hopeful stare and looked towards his feet. "I know the bear skin won't help us much in the water, but we have to try. We have forty days, we can do it. Heidash said so."

"Heidash said we'd die," Mara said.

"Probably," Torniv laughed. "He said we'd *probably* die."

"Probably will be definitely unless you tell me real quick what you're doing sneaking around here," whispered a voice in Torniv's ear as a small knife pressed to his throat.

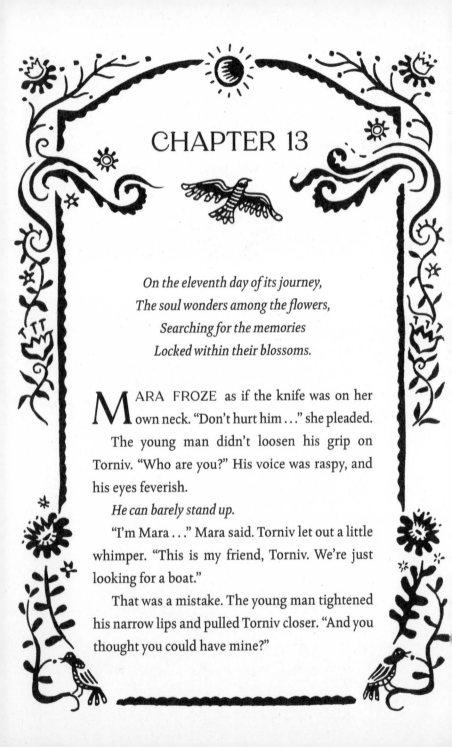

CHAPTER 13

On the eleventh day of its journey,
The soul wonders among the flowers,
Searching for the memories
Locked within their blossoms.

MARA FROZE as if the knife was on her own neck. "Don't hurt him..." she pleaded.

The young man didn't loosen his grip on Torniv. "Who are you?" His voice was raspy, and his eyes feverish.

He can barely stand up.

"I'm Mara..." Mara said. Torniv let out a little whimper. "This is my friend, Torniv. We're just looking for a boat."

That was a mistake. The young man tightened his narrow lips and pulled Torniv closer. "And you thought you could have mine?"

"No!" Mara put her hands up. "That is, I didn't know you had a boat." The man narrowed her eyes at Mara. "I didn't mean to steal anything! I mean, I didn't! I wouldn't! I . . . Please, let him go!" Mara was nearly crying now, which made the man holding Torniv hesitate. He lowered the knife.

"I wasn't really going to hurt him, girl," he said, as if ashamed. "Living alone makes a man jumpy, is all."

As soon as the knife was off his throat, Torniv stumbled towards Mara, his hand already on the bear skin. Mara placed her hand on his shoulder. He understood. The young man had mentioned a boat.

"My name's Alik," the man said. He coughed, pushed his light hair off his eyes, and attempted a smile. He had very white, very straight teeth and a face which would be considered pleasant under almost any other circumstances. But Mara noticed his clothes were dirty and worn, his red jacket dull under the grime and dry sea salt. His clothes seemed too large on him, and Mara understood that this was a man who knew hunger. She knew a hungry man was a desperate one. Maybe even desperate enough to be of use to them. Alik shifted his weight and something about the way the fabric shifted on his chest caught her attention. She sucked in a breath.

"It's good to meet you, Alik," she said, weighing her words.

"Is it?" Alik raised an eyebrow. He sat down on the sand

next to them. "You're a very polite young lady. I've learnt the hard way to be wary of polite young ladies—" He turned away and coughed violently, his fist hitting his chest as if he'd liked to beat at the thing strangling the breath out of him. When the coughing fit was finished, he stayed on his knees for a while. Without turning around, he said, "Why are you two here?"

"Why wouldn't we be?" Torniv bristled.

"You're both too young to be on your own and this one," Alik pointed at Mara, "is wearing threads far too fine for you two to be cast-out orphans."

"We need a boat," explained Mara. "You said you have one. Would you lend it to us?"

Alik stared at her for a moment.

"Please?" she added.

"No." Alik stood up and wiped the sand off his trousers. "But good luck finding an idiot who would." He began to walk away.

"You don't even know what we need it for!" Torniv shouted.

"And I don't need to." Alik said. "But if you wait a bit . . . well, I guess you might as well have it then. I won't need it for long."

Mara and Torniv trailed after the young man. "What do you mean?" she asked.

Alik looked at her with bloodshot eyes. "What do you think?"

He walked towards a tiny hut, hidden among the dunes,

sheltered against the cold sea air. The children followed him and he didn't stop them.

Inside, it was warm but smoky, which provoked another coughing fit in Alik. He collapsed onto some dirty straw bedding and breathed in quick, shallow breaths.

"What's wrong with him?" Torniv asked.

Mara didn't reply. She watched Alik with a determined look on her face. She sat down next to him. "How long have you been like this?" she asked.

He grunted and waved her away.

She didn't move. "You said you have a boat."

"It's . . . mine . . ." An angry look passed across his face but Mara wasn't afraid. When Alik's knife was on Torniv's throat she had been too scared to notice how weak he was. The short walk to the beach must have exhausted him.

"I can pay you to take us where we want to go," she said.

Alik's expression turned from anger to amusement. "Do I look . . . like I need . . . gold?" he said.

"You look like you're close to death," she said. "And I have no gold, nor do I have any use for a boat I can't sail. But what if I could make you better?"

"What do you mean?"

"Mara . . ." Torniv said, startled. She gave him a look that silenced him.

"If I pay you in your own health, will you take us where we want to go?"

Alik laughed, a sad little noise, interrupted by another coughing fit. He couldn't speak but he nodded.

"You swear it?" she said.

"You're . . . serious?" Alik said. He shook his head. "Fine. I swear it."

"I'll hold you to it," Mara said. She stood up and looked around the hut. In the corner was a dirty pot, still holding some fat-hen gruel. She carefully scooped the remains into a bowl by Alik's side and nodded to herself. "Torniv, come with me."

They walked outside the hut, Mara carrying the pot. Once they were out of earshot, Torniv turned to Mara. "What was that?"

"That was me making a bargain." She beamed a smile at him.

"An impossible one! Or have you developed some magic powers when I wasn't looking?"

"*If* you'd been paying attention," Mara pressed her index finger to Torniv's forehead, "you might have noticed the way he was coughing. He's not sick, not really. Not like my da anyway."

"He looked pretty sick to me," Torniv scoffed.

"Because you don't know how to look." Mara shrugged her shoulders. "He moved around, but the fabric of his tunic pulled at the seams, as if something was pinning it to his chest. And when he walked, it was like a heavy weight was pulling him down."

"Well, yeah, no wonder, that's what sick people do," Torniv said, but certainty was leaving his voice.

"Not like that, not this way." Mara flashed him a smile. She strode confidently towards the sea. "But I suppose we will find out soon enough."

"Where are you going?"

"You'll see."

Mara rolled up her trouser legs and waded into the sea, just up to her knees. She waited for the sand to sink back and then carefully filled the pot with the sea water. She carried it to the beach with some effort, the filled pot being a bit too heavy for her. Torniv grabbed one of the two handles and together they carried it to a spot by the house. Mara led them towards a soot and ash-filled space on the ground where someone, probably Alik, had cooked in the warmer months.

"We need to build a fire," she said.

"What's wrong with the fire inside?" Torniv rubbed his arms. "You might not feel the cold but I do!"

"I can't see a thing in there," she said, already dragging some logs from the pile behind the hut. "Now will you help me or not?"

Torniv huffed but went to carry out her instructions, nonetheless.

Soon there was a fire crackling outside the hut. Mara carefully placed the pot filled with sea water among the flames.

"So are you going to be all mysterious or will you tell me what's going on?" Torniv said, warming his hands and feet close to the fire. The evening clouds were rolling in, tinted with the red and pink of the setting sun, and the Spring air bit with the memory of Winter.

"He's not sick," Mara said.

Torniv raised his eyebrows. "So you keep saying! Are we just saying what we want to be true now? In that case I'm a *Tsarevic*, spending my days hunting and riding a silver-harnessed pony. What's that?" He gestured at his ragged tunic with an exaggerated look of surprise on his face, "Is this my new, gold-embroidered kaftan?"

Mara chuckled and pushed him, making him lose his balance. "I know he *seems* sick. But it's just a *Dusiol*."

Torniv became serious again. "A *Dusiol*? That's a spirit of some kind, isn't it? Is Alik going to be alright?"

Mara made a noncommittal noise. "Well, not without us he won't be. If the *Dusiol* isn't chased away, Alik will die." She looked inside the pot and smiled. "Luckily for him, I know how to get rid of it." She used two sticks to pull and nudge the hot pot out of the fire.

Torniv glanced inside. "Salt."

Mara nodded.

The children brought the salt into Alik's hut using an emptied cup. Mara crushed the crystals with a long pebble, till it resembled fine flour.

Alik turned his face towards them but said nothing. His skin was clammy and his breathing heavy.

Mara kneeled next to him. "Whatever happens, don't move," she said.

Alik made a noise which Mara interpreted as a chuckle.

Torniv stood on the other side of the bed, hot embers from the fire placed inside the pot he carried.

Mara took a breath and threw a pinch of salt into the air above Alik.

Alik's eyes opened in horror as the white powder revealed a shape. It was hard to make out at first, as the salt settled like frost on the body of a small fat creature, not much bigger than a baby.

Only the parts where the salt landed showed, but then, as the spell was broken, the rest of the *Dusiol* was revealed. It was naked except for a fur-covered loincloth tied around the fat folds of its belly and a little cap on its bald head. Mara motioned to Alik not to move.

"Good evening, *Dusiol*," Mara said formally.

The creature hissed at her between its teeth, yellow and crooked in its fat-lipped mouth. Once its form became fully visible something shifted, and the *Dusiol* became solid and tangible, his pungent smell filling the room.

"Get it off me!" Alik said, and his hands went up to try and pull the *Dusiol* off.

Torniv and Mara pressed his arms down. Mara shot him a warning look. Alik understood and lay still again, only his eyes betraying his fear. The creature gave Alik a sly look and wiggled his fat body, making the young man groan in pain.

"I see you've made yourself comfortable," Mara said, betraying no emotion. "But I'm afraid I need you to get off."

The *Dusiol*, who up till now had made no sign of understanding Mara, snapped his head around and laughed. "Your needs are not my concern. I found this one. It's mine. And it's full of life and strength and it will feed me long after its bones are rotted in the ground."

"I'm afraid you misunderstand," Mara said, nodding to Torniv, who, with a wide grin, fished out a hot ember from the pot, using two sticks.

The *Dusiol* looked at Torniv and its eyes narrowed into slits. "You don't want to do that, human. You're still full of life but I will feast on all that is you if you raise your hand against me."

Torniv pressed the hot ember to the *Dusiol's* belly. The creature howled in pain, and took a swipe at Torniv, who dodged its short arm with ease.

"I will drink your soul from a cup made from your skull, little boy! I will crush your bones and knead them into bread!" The *Dusiol* cried, red tears streaming from its eyes.

"I'm not afraid of you," Torniv said, though his lip trembled.

"Again," Mara said. She blew a pinch of salt into the *Dusiol's* eyes. The little monster cried out and lashed out blindly. "Now!" Mara shouted.

Torniv had heard her and he pressed another ember onto the *Dusiol's* stomach. It roared and grabbed Torniv's arm but the movement made it shift its body to the side, revealing a long tube, like an umbilical cord, connecting its stomach to Alik's navel. Mara's hand darted forward and she yanked on the tube, pulling it out of Alik.

Both Alik and the *Dusiol* screamed, the first in pain, the second in outrage.

The creature had let go of Torniv and made as if to grab Mara, but she'd already put the end of the cord into the salt. She stood up and took a step back.

The *Dusiol* hissed and crawled off Alik. It moved slowly on all fours, swaying side to side. Its little eyes never left Mara's face. They left the hut, Mara steering the monster with the cord.

"What's the plan now, little girl? I will kill you for this. You and then your nasty friend. I will consume you both, and never leave till you're both dust and bone under my belly."

"I'd like to see you try," Mara said. The *Dusiol* bent its knobbly knees, folding in on itself, and then sprang up, teeth bared, towards Mara. Mara ducked, and yanked on the cord, making the creature roll mid-leap and fall right into the middle of the still-burning fire.

Mara and Torniv watched as the creature writhed in pain. The flames went higher and higher and the *Dusiol* became smaller and smaller, till there was nothing left but ash.

"How . . . how did you know?" Alik stood in the door of the hut, leaning against the frame. The colour had already returned to his face.

"The first thing my mother did after my da got sick was to try to cast the *Dusiol* out of him," Mara said, looking away. Her hands balled into fists at her sides. "She was hopeful. She told me what to do."

"Did it work?" Alik asked.

"No," Torniv said. He walked up to Mara and put his arm around her shoulder. "There was no *Dusiol*. Mara's da was just sick."

Once the *Dusiol* was off his chest, Alik waded into the freezing-cold sea and scrubbed both his body and his clothes, ignoring the weather as well as Torniv's exasperated warning that if he caught a chill Mara wouldn't be able to help him. "To get the monster's stink off of me," he said.

"You had plenty of your own stink, to be fair," Torniv muttered.

Once back inside the hut, Mara explained their situation. Alik listened attentively, his bright eyes focused on Mara's

face as she told their story.

"So it's Navia you need?" Alik said, adjusting his blanket.

Mara nodded. "We need to get there before my da's soul arrives. Then I'll bring him back."

"Your da's dead. You should leave the dead alone. Mourn them, sing a lament, then be on your way." Alik poked the fire with a stick. A cloud of sparks crackled above their heads.

"You swore to take us wherever we wanted to go!" Torniv bristled.

Alik sighed and made no reply.

"I got the *Dusiol* off your chest," Mara said.

"I know what you did," Alik said. He rubbed his forehead. "I'm not a liar. I'll take you where you need to go." He raised his hand as Torniv and Mara beamed at him. "But you might die. You know that. I can keep us safe from the *Vodyanoi*, and any other servants of the sea. I'm a sailor and trained for that. But there's plenty out there to be scared of, and I doubt Veles will just release your da if you ask him nicely."

"I'll worry about that when it happens," Mara said.

"Hardly a masterplan," Alik scoffed. "I sure hope you come up with a better one before we arrive at Navia's gates."

"Don't worry," Torniv nodded, looking at Mara with pride. "She will."

CHAPTER 14

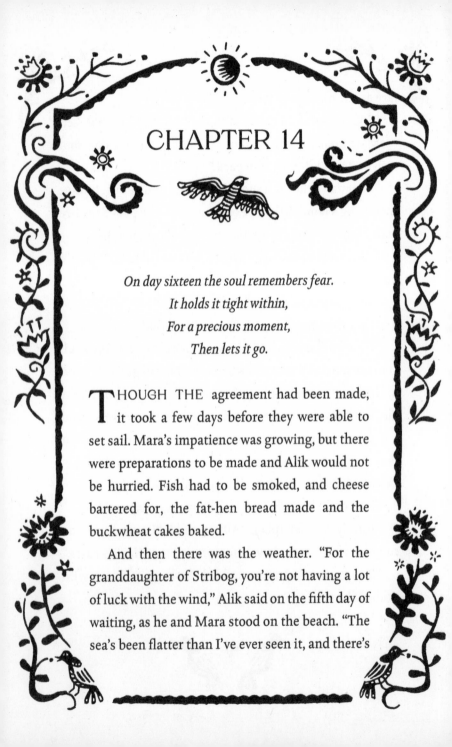

On day sixteen the soul remembers fear.
It holds it tight within,
For a precious moment,
Then lets it go.

THOUGH THE agreement had been made, it took a few days before they were able to set sail. Mara's impatience was growing, but there were preparations to be made and Alik would not be hurried. Fish had to be smoked, and cheese bartered for, the fat-hen bread made and the buckwheat cakes baked.

And then there was the weather. "For the granddaughter of Stribog, you're not having a lot of luck with the wind," Alik said on the fifth day of waiting, as he and Mara stood on the beach. "The sea's been flatter than I've ever seen it, and there's no sailing without the wind. Can't you ask your grandfather for help, or something?"

"How would I do that?" Mara's mouth hung open.

"I don't know, he's not my grandfather," Alik shrugged his shoulders. "Seems to me though, if you want to get to Navia before your da, you need to figure it out, because the sea is seldom calm for this long, unless somebody wills it thus."

Mara crumpled to the ground.

"You didn't think about that?" Alik asked. He leaned down and picked up a handful of dry sand and then let it fall in a thin stream back to the ground. It fell in a straight line, a pale-yellow ribbon. "You haven't noticed there hasn't been so much as a breeze since you arrived?"

Mara shook her head. "I've never been by the sea. I don't know anything about it or what is and isn't normal here."

"If you weren't here, I would probably think it's just a bit unusual." Alik put a hand on Mara's shoulder. "But with you here? Nah. My advice is to sort it out with your grandfather."

Mara nodded. Alik turned around and walked to the hut. Mara sat there for a while, her arms folded in her lap, and looked towards the sea.

After a while she stood up, a determined look on her face. She walked up to the sea edge and cleared her throat. "Viatroduya?" she said in the smallest whisper.

A little gust of wind blew in her face, to disappear almost instantly. She tried again. "Viatroduya? Can you hear me?"

Mara put her fingers to her mother's braid and almost immediately, several tiny whirlwinds picked up the sand at her feet.

"Do you know why there's no wind on the sea?" Mara asked. "Is it because of my grandfather's orders?"

There is always wind, Stribog-kin. A voice like a whistle rang in her ears. *Sometimes the wind stays still, very still, but it's never gone, and neither am I.*

"So why is it still?" Mara asked. She looked around, but Viatroduya was no more than a voice that day, choosing no form she could see, possibly to rattle her.

Viatroduya was possibly the most mean-spirited of the notoriously mean-spirited winds, but he always had her grandfather's ear and there was little happening between the soil and the sky that he didn't know about.

Why should I tell you, the least of Stribog's progeny?

"You mean you don't know." Mara crossed her arms, hoping it made her seem taller. The "least of Stribog's progeny" jibe had hit its mark, but she wasn't so stupid as to show it. A gust of wind blew sand in her eyes.

If I wished to, as I do not, I could tell you, but I shan't.

"I don't think you know," Mara said, rubbing the grains of sand out her eyes. She made no complaint, let out not a squeak. It would only encourage Viatroduya.

You mock me. The voice turned suspicious. *You are trying to trick me! You think I've been in your grandfather's employ all this time and I don't know when I'm being tricked?*

Mara chuckled. "I think it doesn't matter. Whether you're tricked or not, you know nothing! You've grown so weak that you're content blowing sand into people's gruel and passing gossip into Vila's ears. I might be the least of Stribog's kin, but you're the most ignorant of his servants. You pass down nothing, because you either know nothing, or you're too much of a fool to know my grandfather's wishes."

The whistling grew furious in Mara's ears and she had to block them with her hands. *You're calling me a fool? You think I know nothing of your grandfather's wishes? Who are you to say that, when you've received his help and yet he's still awaiting your thanks? You called on him, like some servant, some errand boy, with no prayer, and no gift, though he pulled you and your human pet out of the very claws of Kania—*

The wind quietened and the sand which had enveloped Mara like a curtain fell down abruptly with a soft thud. Mara smiled. She could feel the vibrations in the air around her and could sense Viatroduya's fury. She'd tricked him into answering her question, but he would soon forget. All winds had a poor memory.

Mara turned around, and saw Torniv standing very still, his mouth open.

"Was that your grandfather?" he asked, walking up to her.

Mara laughed. "No, it wasn't him. I just spoke to his servant, Viatroduya . . . You've heard of Viatroduya?"

"Everyone and their uncle's goat has heard of Viatroduya."

"He said my grandfather is angry. I haven't given him an offering after he helped us earlier. I think if I give him an offering and apologise then we might be able to set sail."

"He wants an offering for helping his granddaughter?" Torniv scoffed. "Some grandfather."

"For helping me and my 'human pet', apparently." Mara chuckled at Torniv's outraged expression.

"Stribog is a god. Gods are touchy. You were foolish to forget to thank him." Alik had crept up on them so quietly they hadn't noticed and they both turned around, startled. The young man scratched his head. "Stribog will expect amends."

"But what can I do?" Mara asked, her eyes wide.

Alik tugged on the end of his belt as he looked to the sea. "I never knew my grandparents, but I did have someone like that in my life for a time, and all he wanted was for me to be near, to sing him a song, to tidy his house when his body ached too much to do it himself," Alik glanced at Mara, suddenly embarrassed. "I don't know. Gifts of food are customary as well. Whatever you do, do it quickly." He nodded and left Mara with Torniv alone by the shore.

Mara looked at Torniv. "A song? Could it be as simple as that?"

Torniv shrugged.

"But he's the god of music! What could I sing him?"

Torniv scratched his head.

"Thank you, that's very helpful," Mara rolled her eyes. She looked at the still sea. "Can you bring me some kindling? And a fish or two?"

"Of course, your highness, immediately, your highness." Torniv bowed low and waved his hand with a mocking flourish.

Mara threw a handful of sand in his direction. "Just do it."

"Ok, ok." He threw his arms up and sighed loudly. "But you owe me!"

"Forever." She grinned.

As Torniv was out on his errand, Mara prepared the area. She drew two circles in the sand, and found some small rocks and pebbles, which she placed around a space where the fire would be. She walked to the edge of the woods and found two long sticks, which she sharpened at the ends with her small knife.

After a moment's thought, she pulled out Heidash's flower from a pocket in her skirt and placed it in front of her, inside one of the two circles in the sand.

With the wood Torniv brought her she built a small fire. She cleaned the fish and impaled them on the sticks, which she then propped up with a larger stone, so they'd hover above the fire.

She waved away Torniv's offers of help. "Just let me do it

alone," she said. "I don't know if it'll work but I don't think you being here is going to help."

"But I want to stay!" Torniv objected, growing red in the face. "It's ok, I'm getting used to all the gods and creatures!"

"Maybe. But my grandfather isn't used to *you*." Mara shot Torniv a mischievous smile. "Remember, Stribog is not a great friend to humans. He's frozen too many of them to care if he accidentally turns you to an icicle."

Torniv took a step back. "I'll be at the house then. Alik said something about needing my help. He wants to have everything ready for when we leave."

"I think that's wise," Mara said.

After Torniv left, Mara sat inside one of the circles in the sand and took a breath. She hummed a note, then stopped. She tapped the side of her shoe with a finger. She hummed a different note. She smiled.

Then she sang. Mara sang of missing her father and the smell of the woods, and the sadness at each day's passing. She sang of her hope to reach Navia and of her fear she might be too late.

The words were halting, with no rhyme holding them together. The melody felt right though, and Mara kept time, tapping out the rhythm. She kept her eyes closed but knew the moment when her grandfather had arrived. The smell of ice hung in the air, prickling the inside of her nostrils.

"Good day, grandfather," she said, opening her eyes.

"Good day, granddaughter. I was beginning to think you'd forgotten all about me," Stribog said with a mocking expression. For this occasion, he had chosen a human face, as he seemed to believe his other forms too unnerving for his nearly-human granddaughter. He needn't have bothered. If he'd asked Mara, she would have told him no face or form he could wear frightened her half as much as the sudden shifts of his mood, which she'd seen often enough at his palace.

Stribog sat inside the other circle, a crown of ice on his forehead, and held Heidash's flower between his thumb and index finger.

Mara reached towards the fish. "I thought you might like to eat. I cooked us some fish." She passed one of the sticks to Stribog, who eyed it with muted enthusiasm.

"So you've called me, daughter of my daughter. What do you wish to say to me?" Stribog said. He stared at Mara steadily with his sapphire-blue eyes. He had a long white beard, which twirled and twisted in the still air.

All Stribog said was a test or a trick, and Mara would not be baited. "I thought you might want to sit with me and talk with me."

"So I would, perhaps, which is why I was surprised you

didn't accompany your mother and chose to stay with your human kin instead."

"But it was you who thought it would be a good thing for me to stay there, grandfather. You said so yourself."

Stribog smacked his thigh. "So what if I did? Am I not a god of winds and therefore all that is changeable? Is it not up to me to decide what is right, moment to moment, and up to my kin to listen and anticipate any messages I might send them?"

Mara bit her lip, as reminding Stribog that he had, in fact, sent no such message, would be unhelpful. "I'm happy to go back, grandfather. As soon as I get my da, I will come back, if you wish it."

"And that's another thing! That madness of turning things back from their proper course! Zevena should never have allowed it!" Stribog raised his voice and as he did so, the waves rose behind him.

"I didn't ask her," Mara said, in a voice much smaller than she'd hoped.

Stribog stared at her for a moment. "You didn't ask her?"

"No."

A small pause and Mara winced, anticipating Stribog's fury. Instead he roared with laughter, which sprung icy spikes from the flames of Mara's fire, and brought a flurry of snow twirling its way across the beach.

"You're my blood after all," Stribog said, a smile still

dancing on his lips. Every word he spoke escaped first as a swirl of frost settling on his cheek. His voice seemed to sometimes come from his throat, and when he forgot the form he was in, from around him, the wind currents modulated into human tongue. "You're a foolish child, though, for you seek to stop the unstoppable. Your father was a human. Humans die. What are you hoping to achieve here? Say you bring him back, then he dies in a few years of a toothache or from a bit of frost in his shoe or any of the other countless silly things humans die of."

Mara looked at her feet and picked at their fraying edges of her boots. "I'm not ready for him to be gone, grandfather. Not yet." She sniffed. "I will be ready next time. Not yet."

Stribog played with his beard, wisps of hair curling around his fingers and escaping as flurries of snow. "So you set your course. It's the wrong one, I tell you. Just change it."

"I can't."

Stribog sat in silence for a while. He looked at the fish, still impaled on his stick. "You don't expect me to eat it, do you?"

Mara smiled and shook her head, wiping the tears with her sleeve.

Stribog nodded, "Fine then. This flower is pretty." He lifted up Heidash's flower, which turned silver in Stribog's hand. "I'll take it. And in return the winds will take you where you wish. Whether you're there for them to take you back is up to you."

"Thank you, grandfather," Mara said.

"Your mother's hair," Stribog said, standing up, pointing to the braid around Mara's neck. "It can help you up to a point, but don't be any more foolish than you have already proven yourself to be."

He stood towering over Mara, leaned down and pinched her chin. Tiny flowers of frost blossomed under his fingertips as he leaned down to look into his granddaughter's eyes. "I've had children and grandchildren aplenty, Mara. And after you're long gone, I will have plenty more. You're not indispensable and so I let you go. But you have some value to me. Do not waste it."

Stribog smiled and with a snap of his fingers he dispersed into the earth, as if he were no more solid than a baby's breath.

She looked to the sky where the clouds rolled as if chased by rabid dogs. The waves rose high and her hair flew wildly above her face.

She smiled and ran towards Alik's hut.

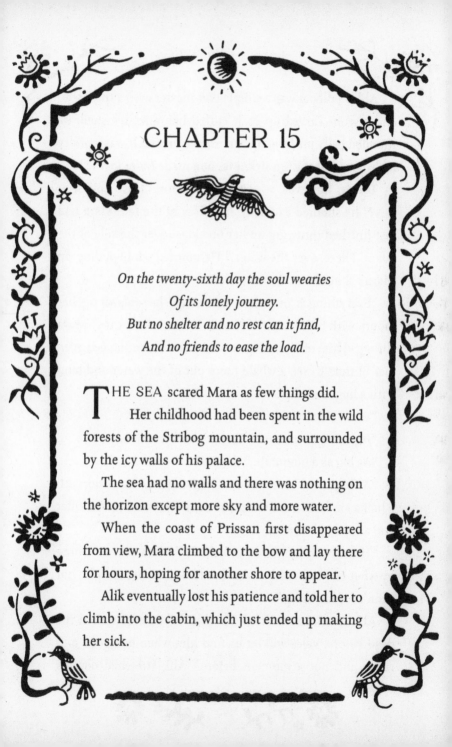

CHAPTER 15

On the twenty-sixth day the soul wearies
Of its lonely journey.
But no shelter and no rest can it find,
And no friends to ease the load.

THE SEA scared Mara as few things did.

Her childhood had been spent in the wild forests of the Stribog mountain, and surrounded by the icy walls of his palace.

The sea had no walls and there was nothing on the horizon except more sky and more water.

When the coast of Prissan first disappeared from view, Mara climbed to the bow and lay there for hours, hoping for another shore to appear.

Alik eventually lost his patience and told her to climb into the cabin, which just ended up making her sick.

Alik's sailboat was a simple two-master with a tiny cabin and a front carved up so it curled like a snail's shell, its rounded belly pushing up against the breeze. It was a pretty little boat, but the sea sickness soon made Mara loathe it.

Torniv, however, was in his element. "Have you seen this?" he shouted excitedly, mindless of the fact Mara had just finished throwing up her breakfast over the side of the boat. "There, over the water!" He pointed while pulling on Mara's shoulder at the same time.

"Everything is 'over the water' here," she said, wiping her mouth with her sleeve. "If it's not Navia, I don't care." Mara shrugged him off, but in spite of her words, she glanced over, just in time to see a whale jump out of the water and land with a huge splash.

"Wow," Mara said.

"It's as big as a house!" Torniv said breathlessly.

"As big as a mountain," she said.

"As big as the headache you're giving me," Alik said, with a half a smile. He was sitting at the stern, hand on the tiller and a rope in his hand.

"How much longer do you think?" Mara asked. "Going by what Heidash told us, we should be arriving tonight, but I can't see anything."

Alik let out a mirthless chuckle. "I've never visited the dead before. Veles will let us find him when he's good and ready and not a moment before." Alik stretched out his legs and lifted up his face towards the sun, soaking up the warmth for a moment before turning back to the invisible point on the horizon which he alone could see and follow.

"That's not very helpful," Torniv piped in. He was leaning over the side of the boat and smiling absentmindedly as his fingers trailed the water's surface. "How can we find Navia if Veles doesn't want us to find it? Is it even a place? A real one, one you can touch?"

Alik shifted uncomfortably. "Your monster friend told you we can reach it in ten days," he said. "Ten days can mean a lot on the sea in my opinion. And the creatures of the spirit world are not always reliable: what's real and tangible to them might be no more than a dream to us. But if this 'Heidash' creature's words are to be trusted, then that will get us to Navia twenty-six days after your father's death, with fourteen days to spare. I don't know any more than that. So I suppose we just keep on West until then." He flashed his very white teeth at Mara, "Your grandfather said he'd help us too, right? The wind's been steady and strong and so whatever you said to him, he's keeping up his side of the bargain."

"He does seem to be, doesn't he?" Mara said. She chewed on her lip. The wind had indeed been steady, and she'd neither seen nor heard Viatroduya or the *Viaterce's* anguished cries in the ten days since they left the shores. This unnerved her. Things were seldom this easy.

Torniv didn't seem to share her worries, though she had

observed him a few times, when he thought nobody was watching, sinking his hand into the thick fur of the bear skin he had stored in his pack, and she had noticed the longing in his eyes.

She had asked him about it on the fifth day at sea.

He'd jumped up then, as if stung. "I thought you were sleeping!" he said, accusation borne of embarrassment heavy in his voice.

Mara raised her head and propped it against her hand. "Well, I wasn't. But I didn't ask you whether or not I was sleeping. I asked you why you're constantly going back to the fur." Her voice was low, so that Alik wouldn't be able to hear her from outside the cabin. Mara and Torniv had agreed to keep the skin a secret for now. There could be no benefit to frightening Alik.

"I'm just checking," Torniv said, pulling his hand away from the bear skin. He pushed his black hair away from his forehead with an impatient expression. "I don't know ... It's just ... It's comforting."

"Knowing you can become a bear any time you like?"

"Knowing it's there." Torniv was playing with the edge of his pack. It looked as if the bear skin was pulling on him, and only through the strength of his mind was he able to resist.

"That I didn't make it up, you know. I mean, do you ever just pinch yourself whenever you forget you have Stribog for a grandfather? That half of you is magic?"

Mara gave him a look.

Torniv shook his head. "No, I suppose you don't. What makes you special is a part of you. You don't even notice." He once more touched the fur. "This is my special thing."

"The bear skin doesn't make you special," Mara said, but then she saw Torniv's hurt expression. "I didn't mean it like that! I mean you're already—"

Torniv furrowed his eyebrows and stood up, at least as much as the low ceiling of the cabin allowed, "Don't worry, I know what it is and what it isn't. I'm just glad to have it, that's all. I'd better check if Alik needs any help."

Mara sat up, which made her head spin, "That's not what I said! I just meant—" But she found herself talking to the air as Torniv had already climbed out of the cabin.

In the five days since that conversation, there'd been a tension between them. Torniv assured her he wasn't upset but she didn't believe him. So, in a way, she was grateful he once more wanted to share the excitement of their journey. And the whale *was* quite impressive.

She crept back into the cabin and onto the bed. The nausea

was still bothering her, and she closed her eyes, willing sleep to come. Suddenly the whole boat shook, throwing Mara off her blankets. "Ouch! Alik?" she called out, but the waves which suddenly rose and crashed against the side of the boat drowned out her cry.

With effort she dragged herself outside. Alik was barking out commands, and Torniv scurried from here to there, obeying, as far as Mara understood.

"What's happening?!" she yelled, trying to shout over the wind. A yellow thread of lightning passed through the prematurely dark sky, lighting up Alik's worried face.

"Goddess Vila," he shouted, barely audible over the whistle of the wind. "She's bringing a message from Veles, though what it is, only he knows." He cast a grim look at the sea. "We'll find out soon, though."

And as if on command, three heads popped out between the waves, their fluid features shifting and changing, beautiful and enticing one moment, and a terrifying mass of teeth and sharp scales the next.

"What are they? *Upiors*?" Torniv asked. He stepped in front of Mara, as if he could shield her from the strange creatures watching them with their cold black eyes as the sea rose and crashed around them.

A spray of water hit Mara's face but she was grateful for it. It woke up her senses and made her forget her dread, if only for a moment.

"That's close enough," Alik said. His shirt billowed out like a sail around him. "*Vodyanoi*—" he said in a sing-song voice, which made the creatures turn to him with an attention inhuman in its intensity. "They're Veles' creatures." He gave Mara a warning look. "Be careful. Don't move too quickly. What is Vila telling us, and what does Veles want from us to let us pass?" Alik's voice rose and fell. *Vodyanoi's* heads moved to the sides, Mara suddenly realised, not in response to the waves but in time to the strange tune of Alik's voice.

The *Vodyanoi* didn't reply, but they shifted their attention to Mara. They swam a bit closer, only their heads visible below the water.

Alik raised his voice in warning and Mara noticed with horror a red welt appear on the closest *Vodyanoi's* cheek as soon as the word left Alik's mouth. The creature hissed, but moved away.

"We were told we'd get to Navia within ten days. We have an appointment with Veles," Alik said. Mara and Torniv barely blinked, holding on to each other, staring at the sea spirits.

"You are close, you're very close," one of the *Vodyanoi* said. It had assumed the face of a beautiful woman for as long as it took to form the words, and then, without warning, a green beard sprouted from its chin and curled around its suddenly wizened face.

"If we're so close, can't you just let us pass?" Mara asked.

Her voice trembled and she hated it. She straightened herself. The granddaughter of Stribog would not be scared. The daughter of Yaris Gontovy would not be intimidated.

"We can let you through if you die."

"We were told there's another way."

The left-most *Vodyanoi* flashed a sharp smile. "Then you can go through if you kill."

Torniv's grasp on Mara's shoulder tightened. "Kill what?" he said.

Vodyanoi shrugged its shoulders. "Maybe the little bear-boy. Lord Veles did not say."

Alik looked at Torniv, puzzled. "'Bear-boy?'"

"And a third way?" Mara said, ignoring Alik.

"You can get something for Veles. A small thing." The *Vodyanoi* smiled. "The stone Alatnir from the Island of Buyan."

"If it's such a small thing, why doesn't Veles get it himself?" Torniv asked. Mara saw from the corner of her eye that he was reaching towards his bear pack.

"The little girl is a child of the winds. That is useful to Veles." *Vodyanoi* smiled with a mouth stretched so wide it touched the bottom tips of its ears. "It is a good thing to be useful. It keeps you alive, being useful."

Alik put his hand protectively on Mara's shoulder. "Where is the island of Buyan?"

"You're not of the wind," the *Vodyanoi* said. "You can't go."

And just like that, a huge wave crashed into the boat. For

a split second, Mara couldn't tell what was happening. The wood under her feet was pushing her upwards, and then she could see nothing but the sky. She screamed, just before she fell into the ice-cold water.

There was a moment when all she could see was green, as the currents pushed and pulled her this way and that under the water. The rumbling in her ears might have been the angry sea or her own heartbeat, she couldn't tell. The briny water filled her mouth and her chest hurt.

Shapes moved before her, darker swirls of green, moving in and out of view. Everything was blurry, and though the cold didn't bother her skin, the ache in her lungs felt like a fire in her chest.

I'm going to see da, she thought and she rebelled against the thought. This wasn't how things were meant to go! She was supposed to rescue him! There was a sharp tug on the back of her tunic, and something pulled her up towards the surface.

She emerged with a gasp and a splutter as her body tried to push the last of the water out of her lungs, determined to live. Her eyes stung when she looked around the suddenly-still sea. There was no boat in sight. Mara's chest tightened in grief. *My fault!*

"Can you swim?" came a muffled voice from behind her.

She suddenly realised what had been holding her up. Torniv-the-bear held the back of her shirt in his jaws as he paddled in place.

"A little," she said.

"I managed to grab the skin, Mara, but there's nothing around to hold onto. What do we do?" He noticed the effort with which Mara was keeping herself afloat. "You said you can swim?"

"A...little..." she managed. "I can...swim...a little..."

"Grab the fur on my back," he said.

Mara gratefully grabbed two handfuls of his fur and pulled herself onto his back, using the bear as a large float. "Thank you." Her throat felt sore and she suddenly felt sick.

"Don't thank me yet," he said.

"Alik—?" Mara was afraid to ask, afraid of the answer.

"I don't know. I kept my eyes on you through it all. The boat just ... disappeared into the sea."

"Oh ..." Mara closed her eyes tight. She told herself Alik knew the danger, knew what might happen. But she knew it was the ice in her talking. Her heart felt heavy with guilt. Torniv interrupted her thoughts.

"Do you know which way's which? I can't see further than the tip of my nose here, and I need you to guide me. Where should I swim?"

"Buyan," Mara said.

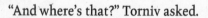

"And where's that?" Torniv asked.

"It's where my great uncle lives," Mara said.

"That's new information!" Torniv turned his large head, trying to catch a glimpse of Mara. "So in terms of left or right, where is your great uncle and his island?"

"My grandfather told me about it once," Mara said. "But it makes no sense."

"Try me," Torniv said. "Because I'm the one paddling here, and you might be light, but even light turns to lead eventually when you have to carry it on your back."

"He said it appears and disappears between the tides. That it's a place between *is* and *isn't*."

There was a moment's silence.

"You were right," Torniv said finally. "It makes no sense."

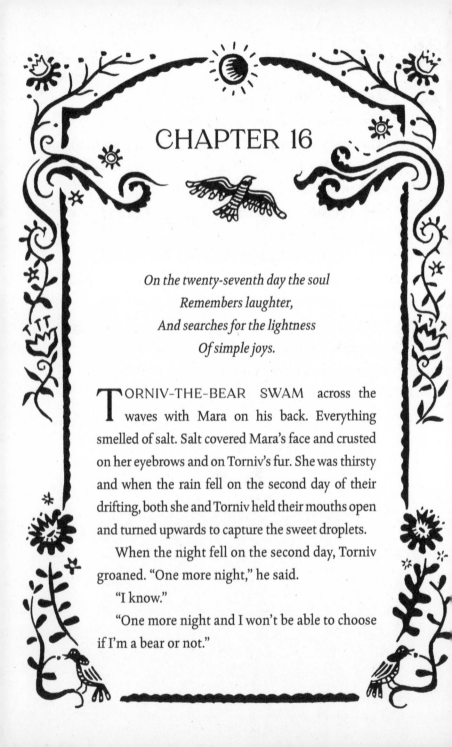

CHAPTER 16

On the twenty-seventh day the soul
Remembers laughter,
And searches for the lightness
Of simple joys.

TORNIV-THE-BEAR SWAM across the waves with Mara on his back. Everything smelled of salt. Salt covered Mara's face and crusted on her eyebrows and on Torniv's fur. She was thirsty and when the rain fell on the second day of their drifting, both she and Torniv held their mouths open and turned upwards to capture the sweet droplets.

When the night fell on the second day, Torniv groaned. "One more night," he said.

"I know."

"One more night and I won't be able to choose if I'm a bear or not."

"I know."

"Solve this, Mara. Even as a magical bear, I can't swim forever. I'm tired." And indeed, Torniv's large head disappeared under the waves more often now. Mara was scared the moment would come when it would not come up again.

Mara had nearly tumbled into the water herself a few times, dozing off on the bear's big back.

She squinted. A warm breeze touched her face. "Can you feel it?"

"I can feel a lot. Be more specific."

"The air. It's warmer."

Torniv turned his nose upwards. "Can you smell it?"

"Flowers," Mara said. She tried to raise herself, accidentally pushing Torniv's head down.

"Hey!"

"I'm sorry," she said. "I'm trying to see. But there's nothing. Only the sea."

"Does it mean we're getting close?"

"Not sure. It's gone now." Mara groaned.

"Call your grandfather," Torniv said.

"He won't come." Mara shook her head. She was dispensable. She'd asked a favour, and had got it and she couldn't ask for another.

"Call your mother then. You have the braid. Ask her."

Mara's fingers rooted around her collar till she touched the soft braid.

"Mother!" Mara called out. There was no reply.

Torniv coughed and spluttered as a wave pushed salt water into his jaws. "Do you think it's because some of her hair is gone?" he asked after a while.

"Maybe." Mara said. "Maybe she can't hear me so far away."

"Try again."

And so, Mara did. She held Zevena's braid and screamed out into the night, repeatedly, till her voice grew hoarse and tears streamed from her eyes. There was no reply.

"I'm sorry, Torniv." She sobbed into his fur.

"It's not your fault," he said. He wasn't fooling her. Of course it was her fault. All of it was.

"But we only have a few hours, and then the skin will become a part of you. Forever. And it's because I couldn't find the way!"

"The upside is I won't be a bear for long," Torniv said. "Seeing as I will eventually tire and we'll drown, both of us."

Mara wiped her eyes and realised Torniv was trying to make a joke. "That is something at least," she said and patted the side of Torniv's neck.

They drifted across the black sea, the long hours stretching under a moon-lit sky.

"You'd think that being Stribog's blood and all, he'd make more of an effort to keep you alive," Torniv said with a huff. "Gods, huh?"

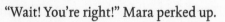
"Wait! You're right!" Mara perked up.

"I usually am," Torniv turned to look at her. "But what do you mean?"

"The bit of the braid I have left might not be enough, but I *am* Stribog's blood! And my great uncle's blood too!" Mara spoke excitedly and rummaged through her clothes. "Do you have your knife? Mine's fallen in the water!"

"Not *on* me," Torniv said with a mirthless chuckle.

"Here," Mara stretched out her hand and pulled up the sleeve of her tunic. "Bite me!"

"I'm not going to bite your hand!"

"You have to! Trust me!" Mara said. "It's the only way!"

"You have a tiny hand! My fangs are longer than your fingers!" Torniv protested. "I don't want to hurt you!"

"Do you want me to drown?" Mara smacked his back in irritation. "Because that's what will happen unless we reach Buyan!"

There was a long silence. "Keep your hand still," Torniv said, a low growl vibrating in his throat.

Mara kept her hand steady. She leaned forward and placed it in Torniv's mouth. "Do it."

Slowly, Torniv closed his jaws, his fang tearing a hole in Mara's palm. She screamed as the pain shot up her arm and the muscle in her shoulder spasmed in sympathy. Then, quickly, Torniv opened his jaws and Mara snatched back her hand.

"Are you ok?" Torniv asked, his bear voice filled with anxiety.

Mara tried to answer but all she let out was a groan. The place where the fang had pierced her palm was bleeding freely. She pressed her hand to her mother's braid and screamed into the night.

A gust of freezing cold wind hit her back. At almost the exact same moment, hot air blew into her face. Torniv roared in fright as the sea rose beneath them in a wave which threatened to crash and set them tumbling down.

Then the wave they rode split into two, and in the middle of it, far below them, land appeared, lush and green. The wave they were on pushed them away.

"Swim, Torniv!" Mara screamed, holding onto Torniv's fur with her left hand as she clutched her bloodied right to her chest. "Buyan is there! Between the tides! It *is*! It *is*! Swim, Torniv, before it turns to *isn't*!"

Torniv grunted and sped up, his large paws moving in a blur of wet fur. The island was in full view now, radiant in spite of the darkness. The moon shone bright over a tall waterfall falling from a mountain central to the island, surrounded by a lush forest. A sweet scent she couldn't recognise hit Mara's nostrils.

She felt tired, so tired, but kept her eyes on the land, getting closer and closer.

"We're almost there!" Torniv said. "Mara?" He turned his

head, pausing his furious paddling for a moment. "Mara!"

"Huh?" Mara looked at him and then at the steady trail of blood they were leaving behind.

"You're bleeding out!" She could feel the panic in Torniv's voice, but it came to her as if from behind a curtain, all the emotions in her muffled. "We're so close! Just a moment longer!"

She placed her chin on Torniv's head and turned her sleepy gaze towards Buyan. The island's beauty was radiant. It shone. It . . .

"It's almost morning," she whispered.

"I know," Torniv said. He didn't slow down. "Just hold on."

"But it's morning . . . If you stay . . . bear till morning . . . Change back!" Mara suddenly perked up. "We'll swim!"

"You'll never make it."

"You can't . . ." Mara tried lifting her head but it felt so heavy on her shoulders.

"It's not far," Torniv's voice grew quiet. He was panting loudly between each word now. "Maybe I can make it."

"You won't . . . The light . . ."

Torniv made no reply. He stared straight ahead as the first morning light hit his face.

Mara felt his muscles tense under her hands, but there was no dramatic transformation, no magic dust falling on their heads.

The thing that wasn't a moment before was now, and it was as simple as that.

She squeezed Torniv's neck and then slipped into the waves as the world turned dark.

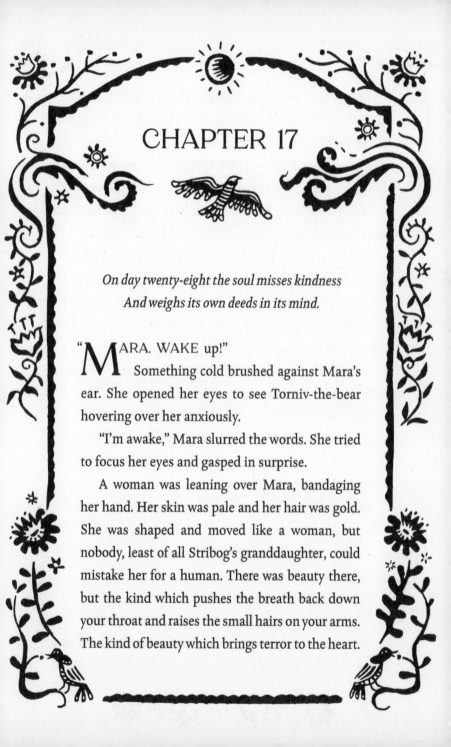

CHAPTER 17

On day twenty-eight the soul misses kindness
And weighs its own deeds in its mind.

"MARA. WAKE up!"

Something cold brushed against Mara's ear. She opened her eyes to see Torniv-the-bear hovering over her anxiously.

"I'm awake," Mara slurred the words. She tried to focus her eyes and gasped in surprise.

A woman was leaning over Mara, bandaging her hand. Her skin was pale and her hair was gold. She was shaped and moved like a woman, but nobody, least of all Stribog's granddaughter, could mistake her for a human. There was beauty there, but the kind which pushes the breath back down your throat and raises the small hairs on your arms. The kind of beauty which brings terror to the heart.

The woman turned her purple-blue eyes towards Mara and smiled. "You're alive," she said with a smile. "That's good."

"Hello, cousin," Mara replied.

The woman furrowed her eyebrows in confusion and then gasped as she saw Zevena's braid around Mara's neck.

"You're Stribog's kin," she said. Her voice was flat, and Mara realised this might have been not a good thing.

"I'm Mara, his granddaughter," Mara said. "This is Torniv, my friend. And you must be my cousin, Zorya?"

"I'm Zorya Yutrenna-ya," the golden woman said. "The daughter of Dogoda, the God of Summer Winds. And to what do we owe this visit, Mara?"

"Can we get her inside somewhere first?" Torniv interrupted.

Mara noticed Zorya wasn't overly concerned about the huge talking bear. The ways of her family were never not surprising. Torniv sniffed at Mara's hand. "She lost a lot of blood and she's chilled to the bone."

Mara didn't, in fact, feel cold, but when gods were in the mood to be welcoming, it could be dangerous to spurn them.

"You're cold? That's a terrible oversight on my part, grand-niece."

A booming voice was carried on the breeze.

Zorya Yutrenna-ya turned around. "Visitors, father."

"So I see, my child, so I see." A man appeared, tall and broad-shouldered, stag's horns upon his head. He faded in and out of view, his form fluid. Mara blinked. It was as if there was a fire burning between them, making the air flicker and dance. Dogoda chose to appear to be in his middle-years, but Mara knew her grandfather's younger brother was as old as the moon, even if his beard was pure honey-brown, and his eyes sparkled blue.

A gust of warmth enveloped Mara, relaxing her muscles and drying the sea water on her skin. She nearly fell asleep from the sheer onslaught of comfort. She pinched her arm hard. There was threat in Dogoda's magic, all the more because he made you forget the danger. He noticed Mara wince and grew in size a little, not hiding his displeasure.

Whatever he thought, he only said, "Your hand should be better soon. My daughter lets nothing die, do you, my darling?" He inclined his head to Zorya who nodded.

"Never in the morning," she said with a half-smile.

"So, now, my brother's grandchild, what brings you to my beautiful island of Buyan?" Dogoda sat with a thump on the grass next to Mara. Even seated, he seemed nearly as tall as Torniv-the-bear. Dogoda cast a glance at the bear and gave his head a sudden rub. "Not the best vessel, that, grand-niece. Should have brought a dolphin instead, ha!" Amused by his own joke, he roared with laughter, and slapped his knee. Warm currents seemed to move under his golden skin, swirling in a pattern not unlike Stribog's frost. Dogoda's daughter stood silent, and everyone waited for him to finish.

"It's nice to meet you, great-uncle," Mara tried to sit up, but her head spun and she fell back down.

"Stay still. You need to drink and eat." Zorya placed a hand on Mara's forehead, more to keep her from standing than out of affection. She turned her face towards Dogoda. "She did lose a lot of blood. And there's a lot of human in her."

Dogoda rubbed his chin, and then, without a warning, smacked the earth next to his leg with an open hand. The ground cracked open and a vine grew out of the hole, snaking upwards, developing a flower, which in the blink of an eye wilted and turned into a fruit, at first small and green, till it expanded, weighing the vine down. Torniv's bear eyes grew wide, as Dogoda picked up the heavy sweet melon with one hand, lifted it high and brought it down to the ground, cracking it in half. He presented Torniv with one portion and then passed the other half to Zorya, who, having propped up Mara against her folded legs, fed her cousin dainty morsels, which she cut with a small blade.

The aroma of the melon filled Mara's mouth, as she tasted the ripe, watery meat of it. It was sweeter than any fruit she'd ever tasted. As sweet as the honey Sorona Gontova would spoon generously into her grandchildren's porridge. The melon satisfied her thirst and her hunger both, and she sighed, content.

Torniv finished his portion and more besides, as the

amused Dogoda grew one, two, three more melons to feed him.

"Now, wind child, you will rest," Dogoda said, standing up. He looked towards the sky with a thoughtful expression on his handsome face. "And once you've rested, we will talk. Stay as long as you want. Stay forever, if your cold wind blood allows you the wisdom." He smiled at Mara and spread his arms. Gusts of wind pushed and pulled at him, like a dandelion's head, till gradually he disappeared.

Zorya stood up too, and made her excuses, leaving the two friends alone on the beach.

After she was gone, Mara whispered, "How many days now?"

Torniv knew what she meant.

"We've been travelling for twenty-six days. With the funeral and all, this is the morning of the twenty-eighth day since your da died." He lay next to Mara and she snuggled against his fur. The sun was high and the air was warm and Mara's tears ran freely till she fell asleep.

"We have twelve days, Mara," Torniv whispered, as her breathing grew steady. "Twelve days and we will make it. You see if we don't."

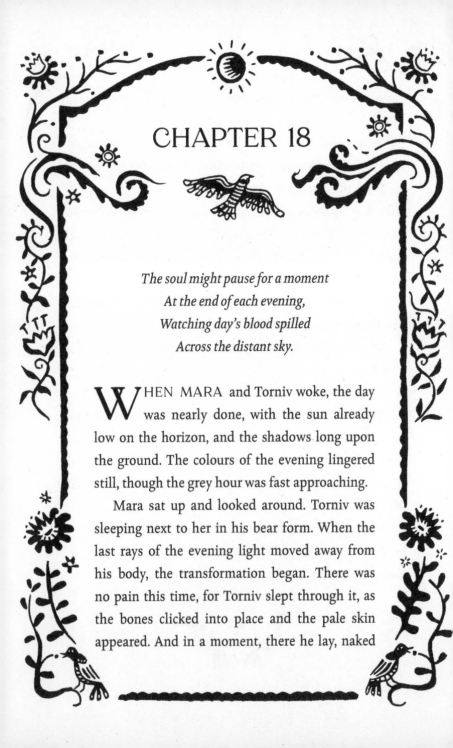

CHAPTER 18

The soul might pause for a moment
At the end of each evening,
Watching day's blood spilled
Across the distant sky.

WHEN MARA and Torniv woke, the day was nearly done, with the sun already low on the horizon, and the shadows long upon the ground. The colours of the evening lingered still, though the grey hour was fast approaching.

Mara sat up and looked around. Torniv was sleeping next to her in his bear form. When the last rays of the evening light moved away from his body, the transformation began. There was no pain this time, for Torniv slept through it, as the bones clicked into place and the pale skin appeared. And in a moment, there he lay, naked

in his human body. "Torniv!" she said, and gently nudged his arm.

"Wha—?" he rubbed his eyes. His mouth was tacky with the melon juice and he rubbed at it in irritation. He looked down and blushed.

"Don't worry, I wasn't looking," Mara said. "How long were we asleep for? We need to find this stone, Alatnir. We're running out of time!"

"I can't find anything while I'm naked, so we had better find me something to wear," Torniv looked around. "Wait!" he said, his face suddenly blanched with fear. "Where's the bear skin?"

Only then did Mara notice that the bear skin was gone. "I'm sure it's around here somewhere!" she said, trying to reassure him.

"And so it is, my uncle's kin," somebody said. A tall woman with long red-brown hair, dressed in a red dress appeared quietly in front of them.

"She has no scent," Torniv whispered, his eyes fixed on the newcomer.

"What do you mean?" Mara was already in a half-crouching position, her fingers closing over a small sharp rock.

"I mean, I can smell nearly everything. I can smell your hair, and the flowers growing in the forest and the sea, but I can't smell her."

"Does that trouble you, bear-child?" The tall woman

GABRIELA HOUSTON

raised her eyebrow, visibly amused. "I'm Zorya Vecherna-ya, boy. I didn't wish to alarm you. Will this do then?" A mocking smile never left the woman's face when a gust of the heady, rich scent of evening-blooming flowers hit Mara's face.

"That's enough . . ." Torniv said, his hand up to his nose. Mara looked at him in surprise. And then it reached her. The cloying, putrid smell of decay and rot.

Zorya Vecherna-ya smiled and the scent dissipated.

"I guess what they say is true, morning *is* kinder than the evening," Torniv whispered into Mara's ear. The woman narrowed her eyes and Mara wondered if she'd heard him.

"It's good to meet you, Zorya Vecherna-ya. I'm your cousin, Mara," Mara forced a smile and bowed deep, nudging Torniv to do the same. She knew better than to insult a goddess.

"My father told me of your arrival. Here, bear-child." She held out a tunic and some trousers. "It wouldn't do for you to catch a cold on the Summer Island."

Torniv mumbled a thanks. While he was dressing himself, Mara didn't take her eyes off her tall cousin, much in the same way one wouldn't take one's eyes off a crouching lynx.

"You said the bear skin is here?" Mara said finally.

"I did." Zorya Vecherna-ya sat down on a mossy chair, made of soil which rose up behind her as quick as a thought and moulded itself to her shape. "The bear is in him now, and not a costume to be donned when the pleasure directs him." She pointed a finger at Torniv, without as much as a glance in his direction. "When my pale sister rises in the morning, the bear will be here."

"Oh," Torniv looked towards his bare feet. Mara placed a comforting hand on his shoulder. "Well . . ." He attempted a smile. "At least I don't have to lug that thing around anymore."

Mara wasn't fooled. She wrapped her arms around him and pretended not to notice when his shoulders shook with a suppressed sob.

Zorya tapped her fingers on her knee with impatience. "Why are you here?" she asked.

Torniv and Mara exchanged a look.

"You're not here for my company, that's for certain," Zorya pressed on. "You want something. What is it?"

"Welcoming as always, daughter," a voice boomed through the air. Zorya rolled her eyes as Dogoda appeared, blown in like dust, bit by bit, till he appeared whole before them.

"Would you ever consider just walking around, like a normal person?" Zorya Vecherna-ya scoffed.

"I'm not a person, my child." Dogoda laughed and kissed the top of her head. He turned to Mara. "I can see you're better now you've had some sleep. And your hand's mended now." He pointed to Mara's bandaged hand and she realised it wasn't a question. She undid the bandage to find the skin underneath pink and stretched, but whole. "So tell me, you

two. Why has my brother sent you here?" Dogoda looked behind him and frowned. His daughter sighed and another tall chair rose from the earth to meet her father's already descending behind.

Mara stared. "My grandfather didn't send us."

Dogoda slapped his knee and laughed. "Come now! My brother is a gloomy one, but he wouldn't let his child-kin travel across the sea to find me. So what does he want this time? Frost in August?"

"He didn't want me to come, great uncle," Mara said. "This was my choice."

Dogoda turned serious. His face elongated till it resembled that of a stag. He leaned forward and sniffed the air, resting his elbows on his legs. "Then a stupid one it was. You reached me because your blood called to me, and your grandfather sent his winds. You were closer to death than a child should ever come. So tell me. Now you're here, what was it all for?"

"I want to bring my father back," Mara said. She straightened her back and glared at the smirk dancing on Zorya's lip.

"From where, girl? I don't have him!" Dogoda leaned back and slapped his thigh. "Though he'd not find a better place, were he lucky enough to stay here. I built Buyan and there's nothing on its sandy shores or in its forests I don't know of. And I tell you, he's not here." The air around grew warmer, the summer god's irritation filtering through.

"From Navia," Torniv whispered. "She wants to bring him back from Navia."

Everyone turned to face him. "Torniv!" Mara hissed.

Her friend shrugged his shoulders. "We need them, Mara. Keeping things secret won't help."

Mara sighed and turned to her great uncle, who sat there in silence, his mouth gaping open. "True," she said.

"So your father's dead then," Zorya Vecherna-ya said.

"He's not dead!" Mara spun around in anger. "He's just . . . I have forty days to get him back. I will get him back and all will be well!"

"Twelve," Torniv said under his breath. He shifted uncomfortably. "We only have twelve days left."

"Ah, Mara," Dogoda rubbed his bearded chin. "You're like my brother after all. He can't let things be either. But it's a mistake to try to undo the natural order of things. All humans have a lifetime each and your father had used his up. His Root Soul will go back into the world but his mortal one needs the rest. What good will it do to bring him back?"

"I need him," Mara said, tears welling up in her eyes. "He wanted to stay with me. He'll come back."

"But this isn't Navia," Zorya Vecherna-ya said. Zorya's voice had grown softer. Mara gritted her teeth. She didn't want her cousin's pity.

"No, it's not," Dogoda agreed. "Did you get lost, wind child?"

"No ..." Mara hesitated. "I ... I hoped you'd help me ..." she said.

Dogoda laughed mirthlessly. "I? I can't help you. Was it your grandfather's joke? Sending you here? No, little girl, I won't help you seek out your death. But if you wish, you can stay here a while. Enjoy my island. And when you're ready to leave, I will send you home. But I won't help you travel West. Not now, not ever." And with that, he left.

Zorya Vecherna-ya sat motionless in her chair, staring Mara down. "You want Alatnir," she said.

Mara kept her face blank, but Torniv was not as well-practised. "How did you know?!" he said. Mara smacked him on the arm.

Zorya threw her head back and laughed. "I'm not my father, bear-boy!"

"Torniv," Torniv said.

"What?"

"You keep calling me bear-boy. My name is Torniv," he said.

"I don't bother learning the names of dead things," Zorya said without a smile. "And what you want, you won't survive." She turned to Mara. Mara noticed her cousin's blood-red dress had turned darker, with purple creeping into the folds of the fabric. "Veles wants Alatnir. He's always wanted that stone. But Alatnir is well protected. And a little near-human child and a bear-boy will not be able to get it, not without help."

Mara and Torniv looked at each other.

"But how do we—" Mara turned around but Zorya Vecherna-ya was already gone. The moon was bright in the unclouded sky, and Mara could see Torniv's face clearly, as he sat with his arms embracing his knees.

"You seem worried." Mara sniffed, feeling less than confident herself. Zorya Vecherna-ya's words had had their desired effect, and Mara was scared, though she had no intention of showing it. "Look," she said. "You've done so much for me already, so much more than you signed up for. If you want to go back, that's fine. More than fine," she corrected herself seeing a dark cloud pass over Torniv's face. "Thank you for everything. And once I have my da, I will find a way to take the curse off you."

"The curse?"

"The bear thing," Mara said quickly. "I will ask Stribog. He will help you."

Torniv sniggered. "You weren't listening, were you? Uncle Borovy said no wind god would be able to help me if I kept the bear skin on too long. I'm stuck with it. And you're stuck with me."

"You heard what Zorya said. You won't survive this." Mara sliced her hand through the air, as if to cut the conversation. "I can't let you die for this."

Torniv was quiet for a while. "Zorya said you won't survive this either." He shook his head. "And the way I see

it, we both have at least a bit of a chance if we go together."

"But I'm doing it for *my* da." Mara balled her hands into fists. *Why wouldn't he listen?* "Your da is fine and waiting for you, and probably worried sick!"

"Yes, he is," Torniv nodded. "And how do you think he will feel when I come back as a bear? Would probably set the dogs on me before I had the chance to say a word. I came this far because I'm your friend. Don't throw it in my face like I have no reason to be here. I'm trying to keep you alive, the least you could say is thank you!"

Mara opened her mouth to respond, when a woman's voice, deep and silky, said, "And try you might, boy, but trying doesn't get you far with Baba Latingorka."

Torniv and Mara whipped their heads around to see a beautiful woman stand before them. She was tall, with hair which fell in thick black waves down to her waist. Her eyes shone in the moonlight, and her figure was full. There was a softness and a warmth to her.

"You're Zorya," Torniv said. "Another one."

The woman smiled. "I'm Zorya Necna-ya. And I know what you don't, and what you don't know can keep you alive."

CHAPTER 19

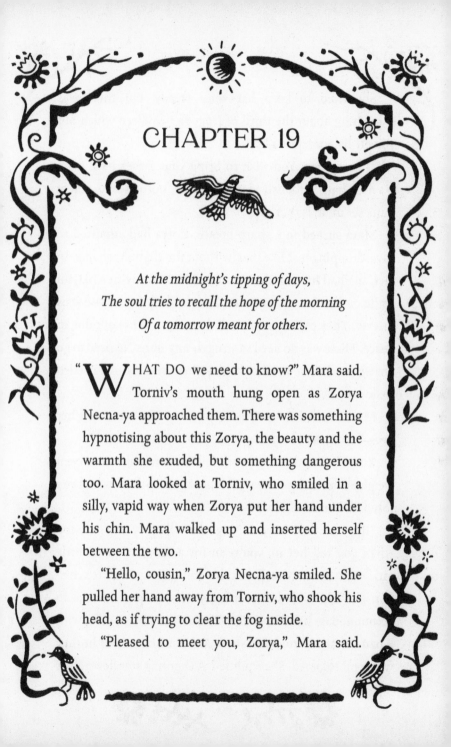

At the midnight's tipping of days,
The soul tries to recall the hope of the morning
Of a tomorrow meant for others.

"WHAT DO we need to know?" Mara said. Torniv's mouth hung open as Zorya Necna-ya approached them. There was something hypnotising about this Zorya, the beauty and the warmth she exuded, but something dangerous too. Mara looked at Torniv, who smiled in a silly, vapid way when Zorya put her hand under his chin. Mara walked up and inserted herself between the two.

"Hello, cousin," Zorya Necna-ya smiled. She pulled her hand away from Torniv, who shook his head, as if trying to clear the fog inside.

"Pleased to meet you, Zorya," Mara said.

She tried to keep her voice steady, but there was something about the third of Dogoda's children which put you off-balance, just a bit.

"I heard you. You wish to bring your father back from Navia. That's a foolish plan, of course, but it seems you're quite set on it, is that so?"

Mara sucked in a sharp breath. Zorya had admitted to eavesdropping just like that, without the slightest shame. In fact, she had her shining eyes fixed on Mara, with a playful smile on her face. Mara could keep looking into those eyes forever. They pulled you in and there was a sense of calm, of peace. There was no need to struggle anymore. No need to go anywhere else, no need to be anywhere else. All she needed to do was—*No!*

Mara pushed Zorya Necna-ya away. She narrowed her eyes. "What are you doing to me? To us? Stop it now!"

Zorya laughed and the spell fell. Mara felt like she'd been weighed down by a heavy blanket, which had now been lifted off her shoulders.

"If you think Baba Latingorka will play fair or stop when you tell her to, you're in for a nasty surprise, little girl." Zorya sat herself on the soft moss. She stretched out, and like with her evening sister, the ground rose to accommodate her shape. This Zorya wore a black dress with a pattern of embroidered stars. At least Mara thought they were embroidered. She squinted. A shooting star flew across

Zorya's dress, disappearing behind the curve of her hip.

"Who is this Baba Latingorka? Heidash spoke of her too," Torniv said. He kept his eyes down, clearly afraid to look up at Zorya.

"Baba Latingorka guards the stone Alatnir. Did Veles' servants tell you why he wants it?"

Mara shrugged her shoulders, as if it didn't matter, though she suddenly felt very ashamed. Veles was using her, that much she knew, but shouldn't she have asked more?

"Have you ever heard of Koschei?" Zorya asked. She looked at Mara as if she could read her thoughts. Mara made her face carefully blank.

"Of course," Torniv said. He looked at Mara, fear clear in his face. "What's *he* got to do with this?"

"Koschei . . . The name sounds familiar," Mara said. "I've heard my mother speak of him before, but nobody would tell me who he was."

"Koschei the Deathless," Torniv said. "Everybody knows who he is! You can't drown him, can't burn him, can't kill him at all. Worse than a *stigoi*, worse than *upior*."

Zorya nodded, with a laugh. "Yes, Koschei can be a bit of a pest, especially to those who oppose him. And you can't kill him, because he, rather cleverly I always thought, keeps his soul hidden away, with a powerful friend guarding it."

The realisation dawned on Mara. "His soul! It's Alatnir!"

The goddess smiled and nodded. "Veles covets Alatnir,

for with it he will control Koschei. He might even be able to kill him, though Veles seldom discards a perfectly good tool."

"And he used me," Mara said.

Zorya inclined her head. "If you let him."

Torniv put his hand on Mara's shoulder. "If you don't, your father will never come back."

Mara stood very still.

"I will do what I have to," she said finally.

"Oh, but you don't *have* to do this," Zorya said.

Torniv looked at the night goddess with barely veiled contempt. "If you knew anything about Mara, you'd know she does. She will do anything for her family."

Mara looked up, surprised. A wave of gratitude washed over her.

Zorya stood very still. "Then you'll need help."

"Can you help us?" Mara asked.

Zorya Necna-ya stared for a moment and threw her head back and laughed. "Oh, child!" she said. "If only I had my dawn sister's hopefulness, perhaps I would. But that is lost to me, much like my sister herself."

"But how is she—" Torniv started to say, but he didn't get the chance to finish his question, for Zorya Necna-ya threw her arms up towards the sky, and her skirts fluttered around her. She rose up higher and higher, and in a moment she was gone, melting into the starry sky.

"What did she mean, Zorya Yutrenna-ya is lost to her?" Torniv turned to Mara.

Mara yawned. "I don't know, but I bet we will find out in the morning." Her stomach rumbled. "I guess we should look for some food, and rest." She rubbed her eyes and turned in surprise when Torniv placed a comforting hand on her shoulder.

"We will get back in time," he said.

Mara nodded, though her eyes filled with tears.

CHAPTER 20

On day twenty-nine the soul takes measure
Of its life's small cruelties,
Which for the first time it sees
With unclouded eye.

"ELEVEN DAYS. just eleven days," Mara said to herself as she looked up towards the green canopy of trees she didn't recognise. She sat up from her makeshift bed of moss and nudged Torniv, who let out a little bear-growl and then stretched with a yawn wide enough to crush an adult's skull. Having learnt his lesson, he'd taken off the clothing given to him by the Zorya Vecherna-ya before going to sleep, and covered himself with his shirt instead. Now as he stretched it slid off his fur and fell on top of Mara's head.

"Hey! Watch it!" She giggled, then suddenly grew ashamed. Was it wrong to laugh when her da was still waiting for her? When there were only eleven measly days left to get him back, and no plan, no help?

As if he could read her thoughts, Torniv bumped his head gently against her shoulder. "We'll get there. Let's look around the island. But first, breakfast!"

"That's all taken care of, Torniv," Zorya Yutrenna-ya came into the clearing where they had slept carrying a wide leaf laden with fruits and little cakes of a fanciful design. "Eat up," Zorya said. She tossed her golden hair over her shoulder and sat herself next to the two children.

"Thank you," Mara said. She eyed the breakfast suspiciously, but Torniv had already fallen on the food, so she shrugged and picked up one steaming cake. It was filled with the sweetest jam she'd ever tasted, and a crust which crumbled as she pressed it against the top of her mouth with her tongue. It was delicious.

"You're not at all like your two sisters," Torniv said. Mara frowned at him, but Zorya just laughed with delight.

"Am I not?" She clapped like a small child. "Tell me, how are my sisters?"

"Wait, you mean you don't know?" Mara said, confusion clear on her face.

"I'm afraid not. Not unless dawn, dusk and midnight fall in the same hour," Zorya propped her head with her hands.

"Do you miss them?" asked Torniv.

"There's sadness there, but that too is the natural way of things. You, my little cousin, wish to bring your father back and don't care what laws you break to get what you want. But I'm old and I've learnt to live with loss."

"Do you know what I need to do to get my da?" Mara asked.

Zorya watched her for a while. She stretched out her long fingers. "I very much suspect I do. But if you wish to get Alatnir, you will need the wisdom of the three."

"You mean you and the other Zoryas?" Torniv asked.

"Yes, my sisters and me, " Zorya said. She reached and scratched Torniv behind the ear. He settled himself next to her.

"And will you help us?" Mara jumped up. "Zorya Necna-ya said she'd help us too, if she had your hope or something like that. So if you help us, she might help us too!"

Zorya shrugged her shoulders. "Alas, little darling, I can't. Perhaps if I had the wisdom of my night sister, I would."

"And how do we get you that? And please no disappearing into a flurry of stars!" Torniv asked quickly.

"I start each day with hope, but never get to see how the day ends. It would help to have the night's peace and comfort. And the knowledge of where the day went." Zorya said. She smiled to herself and shook her head, rejecting the fanciful thought. She stood up and smoothed the pale pink fabric of her dress. "Explore the island, children. Enjoy the warmth and the sun. Who knows? In time you may

wish to stay!" And with that she left.

"I will never want to stay here," Mara shook her head, staring after her cousin. "Torniv, let's look around the island. Let's see if we can find Alatnir ourselves." She looked around. "Torniv? Torniv!"

Torniv looked up with a slightly dazed expression from what remained of the fruits Zorya Yutrenna-ya had brought them.

Mara rolled her eyes. "Come on, then," she said and walked away, followed by a slightly sheepish Torniv.

They spent the day exploring, with breaks taken at Torniv's insistence. "If I don't eat, I won't have the strength to carry you!" he said. "I will need to sleep too, if you want me walking around the forest at night!"

Mara threw her arms up in frustration, but she realised it was true. She scratched her arm. Her skin was still covered in the salt crust from their time in the sea. "I think I can hear water," she said. "If you want to rest, let's do it somewhere I can wash at least."

They walked a while longer till they came across a magnificent waterfall, with crystal-clear water pooled at the bottom of it. Even Mara squealed with delight, as rainbow-coloured fish jumped up and then disappeared under the surface.

"Watch out!" Torniv called out and then he bounded into the water, Mara still on top of him.

"Wait, don't!" She gasped, a moment before they both fell into the water.

It closed over her still-open eyes and she paddled furiously until she reached the shore. "I told you I can't swim that well!" she said with a splutter. Torniv didn't seem to hear her. He stood in the shallow end of the water and shook his back, sending a spray of water all around.

The water was pleasantly cool and Mara leaned back against two flat stones, occasionally paddling with her legs to stay afloat, letting the sun filter through the water and warm her bones. She squinted at the leaves above her head, their rich greens and yellows. A smile she could not suppress stretched across her lips and she let out a satisfied sigh.

Heavy fruit hung above her head, and in a little while she would ask Torniv to lift her so she could knock some to the ground and they would share the soft yellow flesh inside.

They played in the water, splashing at each other, Stribog's granddaughter and a boy-inside-a-bear, but, here, just two children in the sunlight.

They played and they ate, and they napped, and they didn't even notice when the haze of the day fell over them, till the sun hung low over the horizon.

That night, they slept soundly and in the morning they woke to a day as bright and warm as the one before. Soon they forgot to think of anything but the comfortable feeling in their bones and the sweetness of fruit on their tongues.

They spent this day and the next and the one after that too, in play, remembering nothing their bodies didn't remind them of and wishing for nothing but for the moment they were in to never end.

Then on the evening of their seventh day by the pool the winds changed and a different breeze blew.

"I see you had a good day." Zorya Vecherna-ya sat on a large stone, dipping her bare feet in the waters painted pink by the evening sky. "Or seven."

Mara looked at the red-and-brown-haired woman in front of her, and tried to remember why she seemed so familiar. Torniv-the-bear sniffed the air and grunted, uncertain.

"I know you," Mara said.

Zorya smiled, a little sadly. "You've met me, yes. Don't you remember, little child of the winds?" She waved her hand and a wind blew into Mara's face, chasing away the haze.

Mara blinked a few times and shook her head and then her eyes opened wide with horror.

"Seven days!" she said, grabbing her head with both hands. "Seven! Torniv!" She turned to the bear beside her and placed her palms on either side of his huge head. "This place! It did something to us!"

Torniv grunted and lifted himself on his rear legs. He sniffed the air then fell down heavy, hitting the ground with his large paws, throwing up a cloud of dust. "What have you done to us?"

"Me? Nothing." Zorya Vecherna-ya bent forwards and swirled the waters with her fingers. "Buyan is the Island of Summer. There is no place here for heartache and sadness, and the island will push it out of you if it can."

Mara crumpled to the ground. "Four days left! Four days till da is gone forever. What do I do? What do I do?" She cried. Torniv walked up to her and placed his head in her lap.

"You can always give up," Zorya said.

Mara looked at her through tear-stained eyes.

"You could stay here forever, in the sun and the warmth and the comfort."

"I can't," Mara croaked. "I need to save my da."

"Then you need Alatnir," Zorya said. "And you need me and my sisters to help you."

"But you want impossible things!" Torniv said with an angry shake of the head. "The night Zorya wants the dawn's hopefulness, the morning one wants the night one's wisdom, and you? What do you want? The sun from the sky?"

Zorya Vecherna-ya leaned back into the soft grass. Her red dress grew rust-tinged, with purple streaming in small rivulets of colour. "I'm the death of days, though I'm never given the peace of the night to accept it. I get no hopefulness of the morning, nor the wisdom of the night. I get the fear and the sadness of the day ending and the grey hour to spend fretting over the endings I'm yet to witness. I'm in between things, and the end of them too. It would

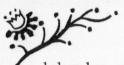

help to have a little of what my sisters have."

Mara's mouth hang open. "You want us to . . .? Wait . . . Is that what your sisters meant? You want us to help you be together?"

Zorya just smiled as the blue light of the evening fell across her face.

"But how? How can we do that?" Torniv scratched his head. "We have no powers! Ask your father!"

"He wants nothing from us. You do." Zorya's voice was growing more distant.

Mara wanted to hold her back, to pull her back to them. "Wait!" she called. She tugged at the neck of her tunic, and pulled out her mother's braid, still damp from the swim. She held it out in front of her. "Grab it!" she said.

Zorya was growing fainter and fainter, but over the magic which pulled her away she seemed to hear Mara. She reached out and wrapped her fingers around the braid. Zevena's silver hair gleamed and glistened in the moonlight, as the night fell. Zorya Vecherna-ya smiled. Still there, though not quite. As translucent as a drop of water, and shiny like a fish scale.

The three of them waited in silence. Torniv, now turned back into a boy, dressed quietly and sat next to Mara, who clutched the two ends of the braid, while Zorya Vecherna-ya held the middle.

Hours passed, and the moon hung high above their heads when Zorya Necna-ya moved soundlessly into the clearing.

The spray from the waterfall settled on her skin, and the air filled with a smell of night jasmine.

"Sister . . ." she said, tears shining in her ageless eyes.

"Here, hold the end of my mother's braid," Mara said. "This way you can be together, outside of your usual time."

Zorya Necna-ya barely seemed to notice Mara, her eyes fixed on her sister. She did, however, grab hold of the braid. Something seemed to happen to the braid itself, as it shone in the darkness. Zorya Vecherna-ya became a little more solid, and the two sisters entwined their fingers on the hands not holding Zevena's hair.

They spoke low, in a language older than humanity, of secrets for their ears only.

Torniv held Mara's right hand, as she was too scared to move.

And so the morning found them.

Torniv nudged Mara with his bear nose and she shuddered awake, relieved to find she was still holding the end of the braid.

"She's almost here," Torniv said.

They both held their breath as the morning light flooded the clearing, though the sun was still hidden by the trees.

"You've done it! As I knew you would!" Zorya Yutrenna-ya's voice carried the joy which swelled in Mara's chest, the surprise of which almost made her drop the braid. Torniv grabbed the end in his jaws and shot her a look.

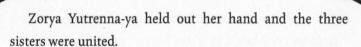

Zorya Yutrenna-ya held out her hand and the three sisters were united.

Mara still held onto her mother's braid. She would let go of it any moment now. She would. She felt the silky texture under her fingers and imagined she could still smell her mother's perfume on it. It was the last thing she had, the only thing of her mother's. But it was the answer, and she'd let go, in just a moment, in a heartbeat or two.

Torniv nudged her with his nose and sniffed at her face. She realised she'd been crying. She let go of the braid and looked at her hand, which felt so empty all of a sudden. Torniv grunted and she hugged his neck.

The three sisters rose up, Zorya Necna-ya's and Zorya Yutrenna-ya's free arms wrapped tight around each other's shoulders.

The three of them were even more beautiful together than they were apart and Mara felt as if her heart would burst.

Torniv-the-bear nudged her. "We have three days left, Mara."

She nodded. "Zorya sisters!" she called out, and for a moment it seemed as if nobody heard her.

When the Zoryas turned their eyes to her, Mara's knees grew weak. Torniv whined next to her. Being stared down by three goddesses was a frightening experience. But Mara was Stribog's granddaughter and she would not cower. They owed her.

"You promised us help! I did what you wanted, and now I need to get Alatnir to Veles before my da disappears in Navia."

"We will help you, little cousin," Zorya Yutrenna-ya said.

"So listen closely," said Zorya Necna-ya.

"And trust only us," said Zorya Vecherna-ya.

The three sisters turned round and round in a circle till Mara couldn't tell which one was speaking.

"When you get to Baba Latingorka's cave—"

"—don't trust what you see—"

"—don't trust what you hear—"

"—don't trust your feelings—"

"—the moon will guide you—"

"—the water will burn you—"

"—the fire will heal you—"

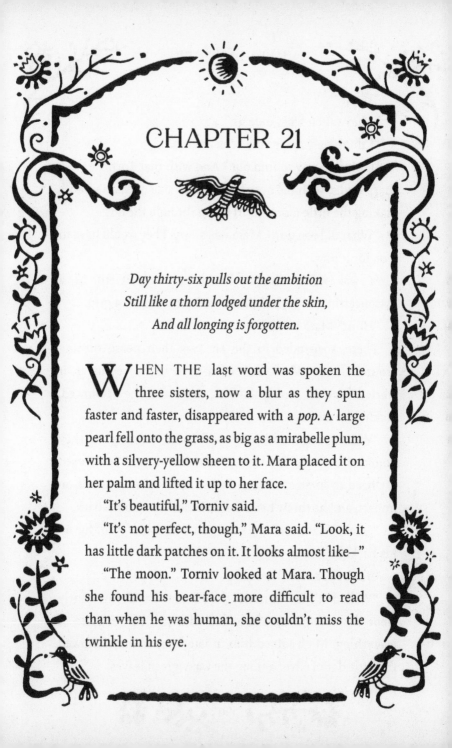

CHAPTER 21

*Day thirty-six pulls out the ambition
Still like a thorn lodged under the skin,
And all longing is forgotten.*

W HEN THE last word was spoken the three sisters, now a blur as they spun faster and faster, disappeared with a *pop*. A large pearl fell onto the grass, as big as a mirabelle plum, with a silvery-yellow sheen to it. Mara placed it on her palm and lifted it up to her face.

"It's beautiful," Torniv said.

"It's not perfect, though," Mara said. "Look, it has little dark patches on it. It looks almost like—"

"The moon." Torniv looked at Mara. Though she found his bear-face more difficult to read than when he was human, she couldn't miss the twinkle in his eye.

"What?"

"They said it will guide us."

"I think they meant the *actual* moon."

"Only one way to find out." And with that Torniv gave a sharp nudge with his nose to the underside of Mara's hand, making the little moon-pearl fly up through the air.

"What did you do?!" Mara was angry. They would have to look for it now.

"I was right," Torniv bared his large teeth in a disconcerting way, which Mara understood to be a grin.

"Huh?" Mara looked up.

There, suspended in the air, was their pearl, turning around slowly. When they both fixed their eyes on it, it started moving, slowly at first, and once they followed, picking up the pace.

"We're going to lose it," said Mara, panting, as they bounded between the trees. Without a word, Torniv used his head to intercept Mara, so her body bent around it on impact, and he threw her unceremoniously onto his back.

"Ouch! That hurt," she said, grabbing handfuls of fur on his back.

"You're too slow," he said.

"Well, don't lose it now!" she screamed as Torniv nearly went the wrong way. He roared with joy, and in spite of everything, Mara joined him in laughter, as they followed the little dot of silver among the waxy-green leaves.

They ran for a long while, and the sun was already on its way down when they reached the mountain.

The moon-pearl hovered around the side of a moss-covered rock, when Torniv came into view, panting heavily.

Mara slid off the bear's side and winced, her legs stiff from the long ride. She hesitated and reached out towards the unmoving pearl. She grasped it and put it in her pocket.

"Zorya mentioned Baba Latingorka being in a cave," Torniv said, sniffing the mountain side. "But I don't see one."

"The moon-pearl stopped though." Mara said. She looked up. The mountain was much taller than it seemed from the sea. "Does it mean the cave is nearby?"

"Why doesn't it lead us right up to it do you think?" Torniv looked around, sniffing the ground. "Do you think it's keeping us safe from this Baba Latingorka everyone keeps talking about?"

"If it did it wouldn't be doing a great job of leading us to Alatnir," Mara shrugged. In her pocket the pearl vibrated gently, tickling her palm. "Better look for this entrance. Can you smell anything?"

"Not much," Torniv said, walking up to the wall. "I can smell the dirt and bits of rock dust and moss and," he paused by the rock where the pearl had stopped, "and nothing . . . Mara?"

"Yes?"

"There's a breeze coming right from this smaller slab."

Mara frowned. "A breeze?" She kneeled down. The slab Torniv pointed at with his nose was just about her height and oval in shape. "I wonder . . ." She reached out towards it and tried to push it. Her hand went straight through as if no stone was there at all. She looked at Torniv.

"This must be the entrance," Mara said. "We should go in!"

"Except I can't fit through this hole as a bear," he said. "We have to wait till nightfall."

"No, I'm not wasting a moment more if I don't have to!" Mara stared at the rock. It was too little time. "I might be able to sneak through on my own. I'll be in and out, Baba Latingorka won't even notice me."

"Don't be stupid!" Torniv grunted and hit the ground with his huge paw. "You need my help!"

"Not if I'm clever," Mara said. She set her jaw. This stupid island and its stupid waterfall had robbed them of seven days. Days spent like some village children, not knowing anything! She stepped towards the slab.

"Mara, don't—"

She walked in. She turned around. She could see the outside, with the light coming through the opening. Outside Torniv worried the ground with his huge claws in frustration, but in spite of the very short distance between

them, his voice was muffled. She turned towards the passage in the cave.

There once was a girl and the girl was me...

The cave smelled damp, and where she touched the wall her fingers came away wet. But she could smell woody, peaty smoke, distant, but distinct enough to follow the smell through the many diverging cave paths. After a while, the light from the outside was too far away to light up the darkness. Mara squeezed her hand around the pearl for comfort. It moved. *Huh?* She pulled it out. The pearl gave a soft light, just enough to light up the area around Mara.

She smiled.

A wordless song rang through the air. Mara tensed. For all their warnings, the Zoryas didn't tell her what she might expect from the mysterious guardian of Alatnir. Was it a witch? A dragon? Mara could hear her heart pounding inside her chest.

"Mara?" a voice came to her.

"Torniv?" she whispered.

"Mara, I'm here! I came after you! I'm stuck!"

The voice came from a space ahead of her.

"I found a different way in! Help!"

"I'm coming!" Mara sped up, following the voice through the corridors. She came to a wide room. There were lit torches hanging on the walls. She glanced around.

"Torniv!" she said.

Torniv-the-boy was stuck inside a small corridor, where he must have crawled in. His head, shoulders and arms stuck out but the rest of his body seemed wedged inside the wall.

"Come here, quick!" he said. "Grab my hands, you have to pull me out!"

Mara took a step and hesitated. "How come you're a boy? I haven't been inside the cave that long."

Torniv stared. "Zorya Vecherna-ya came and brought the dusk a bit early," he said. "Now help me! There was something crawling in behind me! I could hear it! That's why I crawled so fast! If you don't hurry, it will bite me – or worse!"

"I'm coming, I'm coming." Mara picked up a sharp-edged rock three times the size of her palm.

"What's that for? Just pull me free!"

"Stop complaining," she said. "I might have to loosen some soil around your waist to free you."

"Hurry, I can hear the creature slithering in behind me!" There was panic in Torniv's voice as he beat at the rock in frustration.

Mara walked up to inspect the cave opening. "Let me see, the opening seems wide enough. Look, I can even slide my hand down—"

Mara's eyes went wide open. When her hand brushed against Torniv's side, though she saw his tunic and trousers clearly, it wasn't fabric she felt. The hairs on her forearm stood up. She turned around slowly and looked straight into yellow slit-pupiled eyes staring at her from Torniv's face. Her friend's familiar features stretched out in a hideous smile, wider and wider, till the edges of his mouth reached the ends of his quickly-shrinking ears.

Her eyes grew as wide and round as the moon as the creature jeered at her.

"Why don't you help me, sweet Mara?"

Mara was frozen against the rock as her friend transformed into a large serpent, slithering out of the hole in the cave wall. Its head was as large as Mara's whole torso, and it was watching her intently, certain of the kill.

"Are you Baba Latingorka?" she asked.

The serpent's slit-pupiled eyes narrowed. "What is your business with her?"

"She asked me to come to talk with her. I brought her a gift." Mara searched frantically through her pockets and brought out the moon-pearl.

The serpent hissed a guttural sound which Mara understood to be laughter. "Baba Latingorka needs no gifts from the outside, she needs no little girls bringing her things she has no use for. Baba Latingorka would do nothing but peel the flesh off your bones and boil your eyes and eat you in three bites." The serpent's tongue flitted out, as if it could taste Mara already. "And I only need one."

"Wait!" Mara said. "Baba Latingorka will be very cross

with you unless you let me go! She's waiting for me, and will come, and she'll skin you and make you into shoes! She said so!"

"Though it sounds like Baba Latingorka, I don't believe you. You're a dirty little liar and you will be a dead little liar. Dead and gone and nobody, least of all Baba Latingorka, need know it was Lubac the Serpent who made you so . . ."

"No?" Mara raised her eyebrows and pointed towards the cave door. "Why is she standing there watching you then?"

"What?" The serpent snapped its head around, which gave Mara the chance she needed. She raised the flat stone high above her head and brought it down fast against Lubac's head. There was a crunch and the serpent fell to the floor, dazed or dead, Mara wasn't about to stay to find out.

Mara jumped over the long, scaled body and ran to the room's exit.

She threw the pearl into the air and ran alongside it as it whizzed down the corridor.

When she thought herself safe, she stopped, her hands on her knees. "I thought . . . you're supposed to . . . be leading me to Baba Latingorka?" Mara managed. She stared at the moon-pearl hovering in front of her face. She sighed. No point in complaining.

The moment Mara stood up, the pearl began moving again.

A little hum carried through the cave. "What's that?"

Mara looked around, but there was nothing she could

see, except for the yard or so around her currently lit up by the pearl.

A moan came from up ahead. Then words, impossible to make out through the echo. Mara proceeded slowly. She came up to where the path separated. The pearl hovered over one path. Mara opened her eyes wide when she recognised the voice coming from the other way. It was Yaris Gontovy, her own da, calling to her.

"Help me, Mara! They have me! Help me!" the voice came from the left.

She didn't think. It was da, da was here. She rushed ahead. The pearl hovered behind her a moment, only following her at a distance.

"Da! I'm coming!" Mara screamed. He was there, she didn't have to go to Navia, she'd just bring him straight back, just— her leg slipped and she nearly fell down a sheer drop. Mara lurched, her ribs bruising against the stones as she threw her arms wide, grabbing on to anything to keep from falling. She grunted as the sharp rocks cut the skin on her hands.

A giggle came from below. A different voice, no longer her da's, called out in mockery. "Come daughter, come and join me here!" Then a giggle again.

Mara cursed. Stupid, she was so stupid. The Zorya sisters told her to not trust what she heard in the cave. She had wanted this so badly she had nearly died. Her foot found a hold and she scrambled up. She kneeled there for a moment, panting, holding onto her bruised ribs.

"I know, I know," she whispered to the pearl, waiting patiently, hovering above the path. Mara followed it again.

There were no more voices calling to her. After what seemed like hours in the gloom of the cave, Mara once more came out to a large torch-lit room.

A large wooden table, laden with food, stood by the entry. Mara's stomach growled. She shook her head. "Oh no, I'm not so stupid." Heidash's warning was fresh in her memory, and she whispered it to herself. "You'll be hungry, but don't eat, if you Veles want to meet. There be milk and bread in cave, milk and bread will fill your grave."

She went past the fragrant food and gasped. There, in the warmth of a large fire, sat Zevena. She was weaving, a fabric as white as a spring lamb from brown thread.

Mara stood there unmoving. This was a trick. This was not her mother. This was not Zevena.

"Daughter?" Zevena's eyes turned towards Mara. A smile brightened her face. "I've been waiting for you! There's a serpent and Baba Latingorka and echo *upiors* and . . ." Her long-fingered hands flew to her mouth when she saw the state of Mara. "Here, you're hurt!" She stood up and took a step towards Mara. Seeing the girl's hesitation she stopped. "You distrust me. I can't blame you, this cave has a way of confusing the senses. Here, look." She lifted her hair to reveal a shorter patch where she'd shorn off the braid for Mara. "When you gave my braid to the Zoryas, I felt it. I knew you needed my help."

Mara's knees buckled below her. She was so tired and so thirsty and—

Zevena flew to her side and scooped her up. Though she was slender, Zevena was surprisingly strong, lifting Mara up as if she were a baby.

Zevena sat in a chair and held Mara's face to her chest. "I knew I shouldn't have left you. You needed me and I left. But I'm here now. I will do my duty."

Mara breathed in her mother's smell. She felt her mother's skin, cool to the touch. She held a lock of her mother's long hair for comfort, like she did when she was little. It felt just the same, the soft silk of it.

Zevena cupped Mara's face in her hands. "I know you're tired, *moya zabka*, but there's no time to rest. Koschei's on his way. He will kill you for attempting to steal his soul. He kills for far less than that. But there's a way out."

"I can't leave without Alatnir," Mara mumbled the words, tiredness falling over her. *So sleepy . . .*

Zevena shook her head. "Of course not. But I found it, Mara, I found it – come."

Mara followed her, groggy from exhaustion, holding her mother's hand like a toddler, letting her lead her to a steaming pool in the corner of the room.

"There, you see?" Zevena pointed at the centre of the pool. The water was clear and in the centre of it Mara saw a pinkish-hued shell, bigger than a man's fist. "Alatnir is inside. If you want it you need to dive for it. But be quick, because Koschei's already taken flight and we will be hearing the beating of his black wings soon enough."

Mara smiled and looked at Zevena. "I will get da back, mother. Will you help me?"

Zevena cupped her face. "If you need me, I'll help you, child. Now quick, get Alatnir."

"Can you hold the torch over the pool for me, mother? So I can see my way underneath as I swim?"

Zevena nodded and pulled one of the torches off its holder on the wall. She leaned over the pool, holding out the torch.

Mara crouched down and straightened her body, like a spring uncoiling, pushing as hard as she could.

Zevena fell into the water and screamed. Zevena's beauty fell off her and Mara saw Baba Latingorka herself thrashing in the acid pool, as her clothes burned off her and the skin fell off her bones.

"My mother never called me 'zabka', Baba Latingorka," Mara said. "And she wouldn't come to my rescue. Not after I let her go."

Mara walked away from the creature dying in the pool.

Under her breath she whispered the Zoryas' warning:

"—don't trust what you see—"

"—don't trust what you hear—"

"—don't trust your feelings—"

"—the moon will guide you—"

"—the water will burn you—"

"—the fire will heal you—"

And with no fear in her eyes, Mara stepped into the flames.

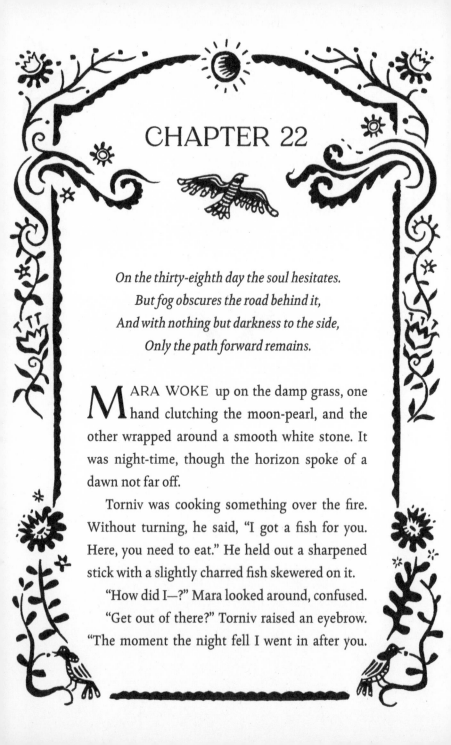

CHAPTER 22

On the thirty-eighth day the soul hesitates.
But fog obscures the road behind it,
And with nothing but darkness to the side,
Only the path forward remains.

MARA WOKE up on the damp grass, one hand clutching the moon-pearl, and the other wrapped around a smooth white stone. It was night-time, though the horizon spoke of a dawn not far off.

Torniv was cooking something over the fire. Without turning, he said, "I got a fish for you. Here, you need to eat." He held out a sharpened stick with a slightly charred fish skewered on it.

"How did I—?" Mara looked around, confused.

"Get out of there?" Torniv raised an eyebrow. "The moment the night fell I went in after you.

I could smell you still, and followed your trail, meaning I nearly got eaten by a serpent. Then I found you, with this stone in your hand." He pointed.

"Alatnir..." Mara looked at it. At first it seemed no more than a pebble smoothed by water. But inside it there was something else, moving, alive.

Torniv sighed. "Thank you, Torniv, I owe you my life."

Mara laughed. She embraced him. "You're the best friend anyone could wish for."

Torniv scoffed but didn't move away.

"Now the bad news," Torniv said while Mara bit into the partially charred fish. "I wasn't able to wake you for a whole day. That means tomorrow is day thirty-eight since your da died. We only have three days left.

Mara dropped the stick with the half-eaten fish. "Now you tell me?! We need to get back!"

The sky began to lighten, and while Mara had her back turned, Torniv took his clothes off. As soon as the morning light hit them, he nudged her with his bear nose. "Hop on."

It took them a day and most of the night to reach the beach. The sea was calm, but there was one problem.

The sea rose in a horizontal wall barely a step or two away from the line of sand.

"I don't know how we're supposed to sail that." Torniv-the-boy said, pulling on his shirt.

"Let's ask my great uncle. Dogoda!" Mara called out.

Nothing much happened. The bees buzzed undisturbed, and the birds sang above their heads, preening their many-coloured wings.

"Don't think it's working," Torniv said. He blanched when a heavy hand rested on his shoulder.

"It shouldn't. But I suppose those who have defeated Baba Latingorka deserve at least a passing notice from me," Dogoda smiled a not-quite-friendly smile.

"We need to get to Navia, great uncle," Mara said. "Will you help us?"

"I did tell you before I wouldn't, you know." Dogoda rolled his shoulders. "And if you'd told me you were after Alatnir, I would have told you to leave it alone."

"I know," Mara said, looking at her feet.

"Oh stop it, no use in pretending to be contrite now. It certainly won't help you when Koschei comes to claim it." Dogoda stroked his beard. His face elongated as he pulled on it in distress. "And for that matter neither will I or any of your kin." He sniggered at Mara's expression. "What, you didn't think he'd be after you for this? Even when you get rid of the stone, the stench and the mark of it will be on you. And Koschei will sniff it out and fly on his black wings and find you wherever you may hide. Didn't you know about Koschei? Didn't your ma or your human father tell you of the Deathless one? Of the shapeless monster flying through the night sky?"

Torniv looked at Mara, "The *Vodyanoi* said nothing about

that! Or about him being able to sniff us out and all that."

"Of course not," Mara said. She stared straight ahead. "Veles tricked us."

"As well he might. He's a trickster god, after all." Dogoda shrugged his shoulders. "In any case, yes, I will help you. But only to get you as far away from Buyan as possible." He clapped, and from the sand rose a large boat, shimmering gold in the sun. "Be gone, granddaughter of my brother. I don't expect to see you again."

"Thank you, great uncle," Mara said, bowing her head.

Dogoda smiled and mussed her hair. "I admit I rather like you. Try not to die, if you can at all help it." And then he disappeared.

"So what do we do?" Torniv eyed the boat with a doubtful expression on his face.

"I guess we climb aboard."

As soon as they did the sail filled up with wind.

The two children grabbed the sides of the boat as it swayed from side to side gently before lifting up from the ground.

"We're on a flying boat!" Torniv screamed, his eyes wide with terror.

"So we are!" Mara laughed. "Take us to Navia, boat!"

CHAPTER 23

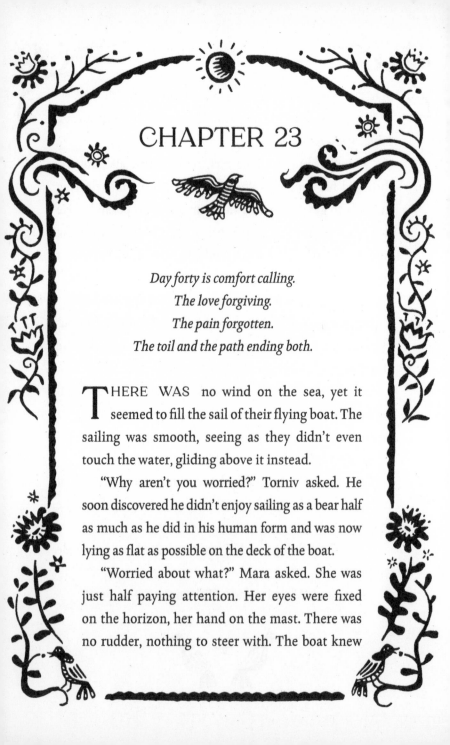

Day forty is comfort calling.
The love forgiving.
The pain forgotten.
The toil and the path ending both.

THERE WAS no wind on the sea, yet it seemed to fill the sail of their flying boat. The sailing was smooth, seeing as they didn't even touch the water, gliding above it instead.

"Why aren't you worried?" Torniv asked. He soon discovered he didn't enjoy sailing as a bear half as much as he did in his human form and was now lying as flat as possible on the deck of the boat.

"Worried about what?" Mara asked. She was just half paying attention. Her eyes were fixed on the horizon, her hand on the mast. There was no rudder, nothing to steer with. The boat knew

where it was going, and all they had to do was wait.

"Well, you know," Torniv said, rolling his eyes. "Just that we're expected to take it on faith that we're going in the right direction, while onboard a boat where we have no control over anything whatsoever, with no food, no water, no idea how long it will take to get there and no plan for what to do when we arrive. We've been sailing for more than two days and most of the night already, and we only have a couple hours at the most in which to get to Navia."

"I know . . ." Mara's expression didn't change.

"Mara!"

"Oh . . ." Mara turned her attention back to Torniv. She frowned. "For one, we'd have food if you hadn't eaten the three melons Dogoda gave us."

"I was hungry!" Torniv complained. "As a bear I'm more hungry than usual."

"In any case," Mara said. "It can't be much farther."

"How do you know?"

Mara drew her lips into a thin line and stood still before she answered, and then the words came out a whisper. "Because soon the sun will be dawning on day forty-one. And Veles promised." Her knuckles turned white as she balled her hands into fists.

Torniv lifted himself up and walked up to her, sniffing the air. "Veles lies," he said.

Mara looked at him, stricken.

"But he has no reason to lie to us now we have the stone," he added quickly. He hung his head out the side of the boat. "The *Vodyanoi*. You remember how Alik talked to them?"

"He sang."

"Right, so can't you do the same?"

Mara looked at him like he was crazy. "How would I do that? I'm not a sailor! They have special training, special words, special songs."

Torniv turned his head to better see Mara and stared at her with his black bear eyes. "Isn't Stribog the God of Music as well as the rest of it?"

Mara hesitated.

"Seems to me," Torniv said, "that now's the time to try. Because in a very short while there will be no more chances."

Mara walked up to the bow of the boat. The morning would soon be on its way, painting the sea orange and pink. She opened her mouth then closed it again. It was stupid. She looked at Torniv who nodded in encouragement.

Then she sang.

At first there was little change in the sea. "Keep trying," Torniv said. "I can smell something."

And in a moment another song joined Mara's.

A head bobbed up on the horizon. Then another. Two *Vodyanoi* opened their mouths and sang with her.

Mara smacked Torniv who'd crept up to her and was dangerously close to the edge of the boat. He let out a growl.

"What was that for?!"

"You're so close to the edge you might fall! Careful, they're dangerous!"

Torniv looked around and took a quick step back. He sat on his haunches, momentarily embarrassed. "I know they're dangerous, you don't have to tell me they're dangerous," he muttered.

"Right!" Mara scoffed and turned her attention back to the *Vodyanoi* who were now swimming alongside the boat.

"Hello!" she called out and instantly felt stupid. The *Vodyanoi* just watched her with a mildly contemptuous look.

"I have the thing Veles asked for! Now take us to Navia!" she said.

The creatures exchanged a look. One of them opened a mouth filled with no fewer than three rows of needle-sharp teeth. "All you have to do is come to us!"

"Fat chance!" Torniv said. "She hasn't gone through it all to let you drown her!" He added, "And neither have I!"

The *Vodyanoi* laughed. "If it calms your heart, you have this promise, we will keep you two safe all the way to Navia."

"I don't know if I belie—" Torniv started to say when he heard a splash. He rolled his eyes. "Damn it!"

And then he followed Mara into the water, straight into the *Vodyanoi's* arms.

CHAPTER 24

Navia is the home of goodbyes.
To the dreams.
To the heart.
To the name.

THE *VODYANOI* pulled Mara and Torniv below the water.

Mara and Torniv held their breath till their lungs were ready to burst, clawing at the creatures pulling them along.

"Stop it," the *Vodyanoi* holding Mara said. She gasped in surprise.

"I can hear you!" she said. "I can breathe! Torniv, we can breathe!"

"Only while we're holding you, so don't get any ideas!" The *Vodyanoi* holding Torniv said, giving Torniv a dark look. "In any case, we're here."

Mara opened her eyes wide. "It's magnificent!"

Navia loomed before them, a large palace of pearl and bone. Magnificent coral gardens cascaded down its walls with multicoloured sea anemones flowing gently, and shoals of rainbow-coloured fish swimming in and out of view.

Mara looked at Torniv, her face glowing. "We did it, Torniv! We really did it!"

Torniv-the-bear grunted, his large body moving awkwardly in the water. "I have to admit, I didn't think it would be so wet."

But Mara didn't hear. She was looking towards the palace, her heart beating fast, so fast she brought her hand to her chest as if she could still it. *Here it is.* And her father would be inside it, waiting. She imagined his joy, his relief. "I knew you'd come for me, *zabka*," is what he'd tell her.

She'd saved him.

The *Vodyanoi* brought Mara and Torniv to what appeared to be a large gate. The water creatures unceremoniously pushed the two through the entrance. Mara and Torniv fell hard, as the inside of the palace seemed to be separate from the sea, with a wall of water at the gate and cold air within the walls. Mara stood up, her clothes and hair dripping onto the bone-white floor.

Her face lit up when she saw another surprise was waiting for them.

"Alik!" Mara called out. She laughed out loud and ran up

to the young sailor, who pulled his hat off and waved it above his head.

Alik was indeed sitting on top of his boat, eating a strange looking fruit.

"You took your time!" he called out. Mara gave Alik a big hug.

"Are you done then? Shall we go back?" Alik asked with a smile. "Where's your da? And . . ." He raised his eyebrows. "Torniv, why are you naked?"

Mara turned around. "No!"

Torniv was indeed standing there in his human form, as surprised as she was. "Mara, the day's done! Quick! Inside!"

Mara ran inside the cavernous hall, where the walls were covered with luminescent algae, lighting up the way.

"Veles!" she screamed. "VELES!"

"You'd do well to learn some respect, child." A low voice came from the other end of the hall. It wasn't loud. It belonged to one who never had to raise their voice to be heard or to be obeyed. "You do not get to summon me."

"I've got it!" Mara screamed. She reached inside her pocket and wrapped her hand around Koschei's soul. "I have Alatnir! Now give me back my father."

"Your father?" Veles raised one eyebrow. He chose the form of a young man, beardless still, with skin of pale green and hair of flaming gold. He was beautiful, but Mara wasn't fooled. He was beautiful much like a dragon was beautiful:

all fire and no pity. "I suppose you did mention something about that. Give me the stone."

Mara held the stone behind her back. Veles frowned.

"I'm not accustomed to repeating myself."

"Give me my father back. Then you can have Koschei's soul!" she said. Mara didn't look away. She stared into Veles' eyes. She wouldn't flinch.

Veles seemed impressed. "So you know its purpose? Oh, very well, then!" Veles frowned. He clicked his fingers. Nothing happened. "Oh dear," he said. "It would appear you're too late."

"No." Mara shook her head.

"For forty days, your father travelled. And now his human soul is indeed safely in my halls, yet his Root Soul's already gone to Veeray, where my brother Perun will send it on to begin life anew."

"No!" Mara kept shaking her head. Tears were streaming down her face. She couldn't be too late! She couldn't!

Veles took a step towards her. "Look up, child."

Mara looked up, though her vision was blurred. Up the walls of the hall snaked large roots, and through the roof grew a tree, larger than anything she'd ever seen.

"These are the roots of Veeray, the tree of life. In its crown roost the birds bred by Sudiki. They each will carry the Root part of the human soul to a newborn child. That immortal part of you gets a chance to be reborn, while the

human part travels to the stars. Unless you reunite the two, well, your father will be your father no more."

Mara looked up. Torniv walked up to her and placed his hand on her shoulder. "It's done, Mara. You've done all you could . . . I'm so sorry."

"No!" Mara turned to him. "I can still get him. His immortal soul went up the tree. Very well. I'll climb it."

Veles laughed. "I'm impressed with your determination, child, but you will fail. Now, Alatnir."

"First, give me your promise," Mara narrowed her eyes. "You will give me my father's human soul as soon as I get the immortal part. The Root part."

"This is not a negotiation," Veles said, and anger showed in his voice.

"Then you don't get Alatnir."

Veles sighed. "Very well child. If you give me Alatnir, I will release your father's mortal soul. A soul for a soul is a good bargain, I think."

"And my friends go free!" Mara said.

Veles nodded.

"No!" Torniv looked at Mara. "I'm not leaving you now!"

Mara turned to him, "Thank you, Torniv. I will come back with my da. But you need to go with Alik."

"Why?" Torniv said. "You need me!"

"I do," Mara nodded. "That's why I can't have you die up there." She wrapped her arms around Torniv and planted a kiss on his cheek. "Get Alik back safe."

Torniv opened his mouth to protest, but Veles snapped his fingers and a couple of *Vodyanoi* entered the hall, grabbing the struggling Torniv's arms. Mara nodded at Alik, who bowed with respect, before turning on his heel and leaving after the screaming Torniv.

"Well?" Veles said. "I've been more than patient." He tried to appear calm and dignified, but Mara could see the greedy expression in his eyes. "What does it look like? Is it as black as his wings? I always wondered," Veles chuckled to himself.

Mara hesitated. She reached into her pocket and fished something out.

Then she dropped the moon-pearl into Veles' outstretched hand.

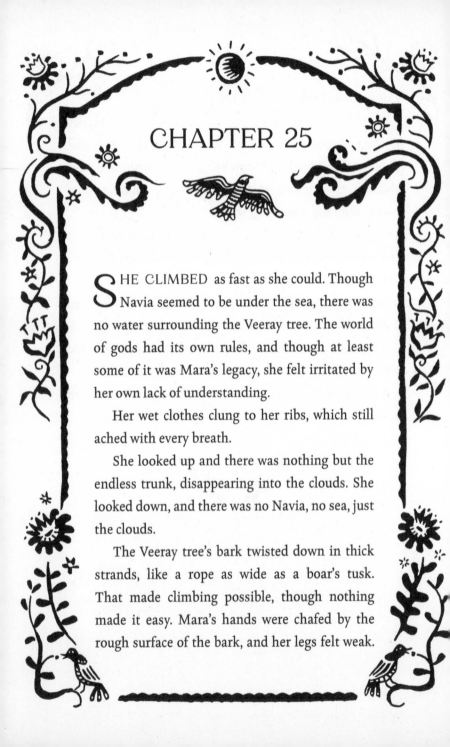

CHAPTER 25

SHE CLIMBED as fast as she could. Though Navia seemed to be under the sea, there was no water surrounding the Veeray tree. The world of gods had its own rules, and though at least some of it was Mara's legacy, she felt irritated by her own lack of understanding.

Her wet clothes clung to her ribs, which still ached with every breath.

She looked up and there was nothing but the endless trunk, disappearing into the clouds. She looked down, and there was no Navia, no sea, just the clouds.

The Veeray tree's bark twisted down in thick strands, like a rope as wide as a boar's tusk. That made climbing possible, though nothing made it easy. Mara's hands were chafed by the rough surface of the bark, and her legs felt weak.

She rested awhile where a knot in the tree created a comfortable hollow.

Mara looked at her hands. Was she wrong to leave Torniv with Alik? She couldn't let him risk himself for her again. After all he'd done for her, she loved him best in the world after da. She wouldn't lose him. But would he understand? She very much doubted it. He'd be far more likely to rage and curse her for being the disloyal friend that she was.

She pulled out Alatnir and held it on her open palm. Was it true what Dogoda said? Would Koschei be searching for her now? If so, she had a much greater chance of surviving if she didn't give away the very thing he was after. And Veles tricked her. She set her mouth into a line. He could have brought her to him any time he chose. He *wanted* her to miss that last sunset.

She closed her eyes tight.

There once was a girl and the girl was me . . . Here was her great adventure, her hero story she'd wanted so much.

She wriggled her toes inside her boots. Her feet were cramping from the long climb. It was still dark, though she could see well enough in the moonlight.

She sighed and started climbing again. She was so tired. It was getting harder and harder to hold onto the bark, slippery from the mist.

Her hand reached for the handhold, which crumbled under her fingers. Mara glued her whole body to the surface

of the tree, but her foot, no longer secure, began slipping too. She yelped in pain as her chest knocked against the hard wood. Her palms were sweaty and her boots had no grip.

She was going to fall.

She fell.

She—

She was flying through the sky, huge talons wrapped around her waist.

All she saw were feathers as the world turned black.

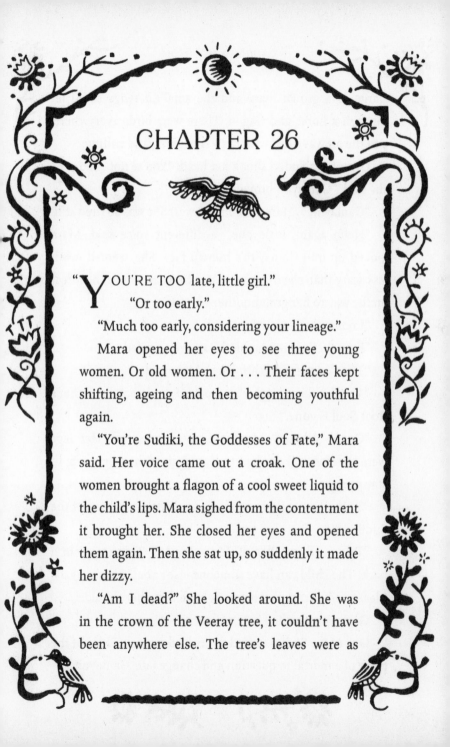

CHAPTER 26

"YOU'RE TOO late, little girl."

"Or too early."

"Much too early, considering your lineage."

Mara opened her eyes to see three young women. Or old women. Or . . . Their faces kept shifting, ageing and then becoming youthful again.

"You're Sudiki, the Goddesses of Fate," Mara said. Her voice came out a croak. One of the women brought a flagon of a cool sweet liquid to the child's lips. Mara sighed from the contentment it brought her. She closed her eyes and opened them again. Then she sat up, so suddenly it made her dizzy.

"Am I dead?" She looked around. She was in the crown of the Veeray tree, it couldn't have been anywhere else. The tree's leaves were as large as a grown man, and the smallest twigs could let through a horse and wagon. There were birds everywhere, and the air was filled with their squeaking and trilling.

One of the Sudiki shook her head. "You're not dead yet," she said. "Gamayun brought you."

"Gamayun?" Mara rubbed her eyes. She was so tired still.

"Hello again, little one," a different voice said. Mara looked up into Gamayun's human face. She seemed much less scary than she did when Mara first saw her in the forest on the way to her grandmother's house.

"I remember you," Mara said.

"I'm told I'm memorable." Gamayun smiled.

"Thank you for catching me," Mara said.

"The Sudiki are right. You're here too late. Your father's Root Soul is gone."

"Gone? Where?" Mara attempted to stand. Her legs were shaking and she had to lean against the tree's twig to stay upright.

"To the new child in need of a soul, little one," one of the Sudiki said.

"Take me there! Please!" Mara shouted. "I have to get him back! The child can have someone else's soul! That's *my* da! Please!" She crumpled down, sobs shaking her shoulders.

Gamayun watched her in silence.

One of the Sudiki turned to the bird-woman. "It's not the place of a mortal to question and change fate, Gamayun."

"But she's not fully mortal, is she? She's in between the worlds, and yet given not a chance to choose for herself which parts she wants of each side."

"She's not *you*, Gamayun," another Sudiki said. "Don't help her because you're lost as well."

Gamayun hopped towards the crying Mara. The girl looked up at the bird-woman. There was pity in the creature's eyes. "But what am I if I can't claim the kinship of half-things, of the lost ones?" She reached out one powerful arm to Mara. "Climb on if you would get your father," she said.

Mara nodded and let Gamayun hoist her up.

They flew with a speed far surpassing anything Mara had ever experienced. Gamayun was faster than Torniv as a bear, faster than her grandfather's ice horses. Perhaps even faster than her grandfather, though that last thought was a very small and quiet one.

The air was cold, and little icicles formed on Mara's lashes.

"Look down, little one. You will have never seen such a sight," Gamayun said. And indeed, under them a sea of green forests and yellowing fields came into view. The Spring had arrived, and the whole world was awaking.

"Everything seems so small," Mara said.

"Yes, a lot of big heartbreaks can go unnoticed from a

distance," Gamayun said. "And there's one coming soon."

"What do you mean?" Mara said. "Whose?"

Gamayun didn't answer.

They landed in the courtyard of a small peasant house. Its owners seemed well off, as far as these things go, for there were ducks and chickens pecking good seed in the enclosure, and a cow was mooing in the barn.

Gamayun helped Mara down and gestured to the window.

Mara walked up. Was her da there? Would she know him?

There was laughter coming from inside the *izba*, with many voices talking over each other, and a clinking of glasses, and laughter. Somebody played a flute, and somebody else clapped in time. The window was open, but it was so high Mara had to stand on tiptoes to look in.

There, inside the room, a young woman lay on the narrow bench bed. Some over-solicitous hands had covered her with so many blankets and furs it was a miracle she could still breathe. And in her arms, with a face framed by a white, embroidered hat, lay a little baby.

"Da..." Mara whispered. The baby made gurgling noises, and seemed to look at nothing in particular, occasionally fixing its blue eyes on its mother.

The mother was talking to an elderly woman sitting on

a stool by her bedside. The old woman was laughing and patting the younger woman's hand.

Mara held her breath as the baby seemed to turn its head towards her. Unseeing, but listening intently.

"He knows me . . . Gamayun, he knows me," Mara whispered. She turned to the bird-woman with a bright smile. "I did it! I can bring him back! What do I do? How can I get him back?"

"It's simple." Gamayun looked at her for a moment. "All you have to do is kill the child."

Mara stared. "What? I can't do that!" She shook her head. "There must be another way! There's always another way!"

"Not here."

"But . . ." Mara looked back inside the *izba*. The baby's mother brought its face to her breast, and the baby began to drink, the fingers of his little pink hand wrapped tight around his mother's index finger.

She turned to Gamayun, fury flashing in her eyes. "Tell me the way!"

"I have."

"No, no, it's a lie! A nasty lie!" She threw herself towards Gamayun, her small fists beating at the creature's chest. "You're tricking me! You work for Veles! Or Koschei, or somebody, *somebody* who doesn't want me to get my da back!" Her eyes were streaming and sobs shook her chest. It couldn't be. Not after all she'd been through. This wasn't

supposed to happen. It wasn't supposed to just *end*.

Gamayun put her large arms around Mara, holding her close.

"It's not fair," Mara said, her voice breaking.

"No. No, it's not," Gamayun said.

Mara pushed Gamayun away and crawled towards the window. She looked again at the baby's face.

Her shoulders shook with silent sobs. "I've failed him . . ." she whispered.

"You've been very brave," Gamayun placed her hand on Mara's back. "You've been very clever."

"None of it matters!" Mara snapped at Gamayun. "I failed him." She wiped at her eyes impatiently, even as more tears kept rolling down her cheeks.

"Look at him again." Gamayun shook her head.

Mara looked at the baby inside. Its father had picked it up and was showering its head with kisses. The baby sighed, satisfied, warm, loved.

"He'll be happy?" Mara whispered.

"That is not a promise I can make, little one." Gamayun brought her face close to Mara's and gently wiped away the girl's tears. "But I believe so. He is exactly where he is meant to be."

Mara looked up at the bird woman's face and attempted to smile. Her lip trembled and she fell forward, allowing Gamayun to envelop her in her arms as she cried.

They stood there in silence for a while, Gamayun stroking Mara's head.

"Child . . . child?"

Mara looked up into the worried-looking Gamayun's face. "What?"

"Your hair . . . It's turning silver . . ."

Mara grabbed a lock of her hair. Indeed, the colour was draining from it. The skin on her hand was losing its tint as well, turning into the pale icy blue of her mother's kin.

"What's happening to me?" Mara said in a little whisper.

"What did you promise Veles?" There was an urgency in Gamayun's voice. "What did you say to him?"

"I gave him . . . He thought he was getting Koschei's soul from me," Mara said and clapped her hand over her mouth. "He said 'a soul for a soul' . . ."

"And he's getting one," Gamayun said.

"But . . . But my da is still dead!"

"Only because you made the right choice," Gamayun shook her head. "The deal with Veles still stands. I'm sorry, wind child."

CHAPTER 27

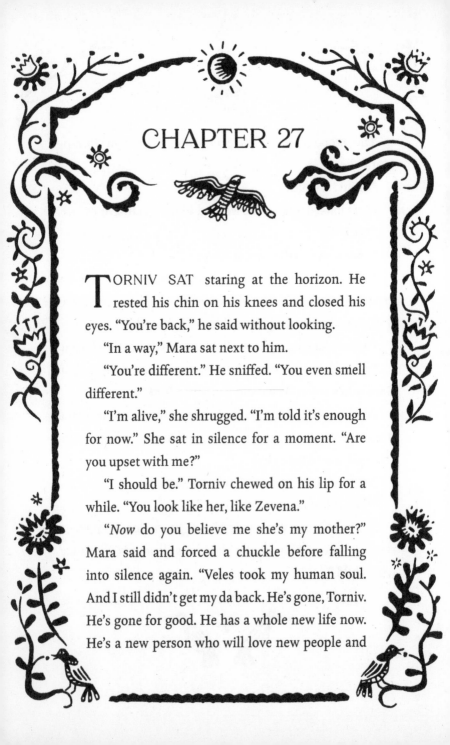

TORNIV SAT staring at the horizon. He rested his chin on his knees and closed his eyes. "You're back," he said without looking.

"In a way," Mara sat next to him.

"You're different." He sniffed. "You even smell different."

"I'm alive," she shrugged. "I'm told it's enough for now." She sat in silence for a moment. "Are you upset with me?"

"I should be." Torniv chewed on his lip for a while. "You look like her, like Zevena."

"*Now* do you believe me she's my mother?" Mara said and forced a chuckle before falling into silence again. "Veles took my human soul. And I still didn't get my da back. He's gone, Torniv. He's gone for good. He has a whole new life now. He's a new person who will love new people and

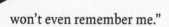

won't even remember me."

Torniv held her hand. "He will remember you. You're kind of hard to forget."

She sniffed.

"So how come you're not dead?" Torniv asked. "If they took your human soul."

"Looks like my grandfather has equipped me with a spare one. I'm . . . different now though."

"So what happens now?" Torniv asked.

"Koschei will be after me," she shrugged. "He won't stop. So I guess I have to prepare myself for him. Somehow." She lifted her face. A whisper ran on the waves. Was it her imagination? Or maybe it was Viatroduya, laughing at the hunted little girl.

"Very well," Torniv stood up and brushed the sand off his trousers. "Let's go."

Mara stared. "Go where?"

"We need to get your soul back. And defeat Koschei. Whichever you like first." Torniv sent her a bright smile. He reached out to help Mara up.

She smiled and took his hand.

ACKNOWLEDGEMENTS

This book is in your hands thanks to the love, support and help I have been lucky to receive from so many people. No woman is an island, and I would like to thank all those who have helped me along the way.

My husband Cameron and my two brilliant, funny, kind daughters, Scarlett and Sienna.

My family, in Poland and in the UK. I love you all.

My writing buddies, Nadia Idle and Rachael Twumasi-Corson, whose company and wisdom I depend on.

My wonderful agent, John Baker, whose enthusiasm matches my own, and whose faith spurs me on. Also Lorna Hemingway, Sarah McDonnell and everyone else at Bell Lomax Moreton.

Caroline Hardaker, my dear friend and my Bookish Take channel co-host. Our chats mean more than you know!

Hazel Holmes at UCLan Publishing, I'm so happy *The Wind Child* found a home with you!

Also to Kieran Baker, whose meticulous editorial work and comments I found invaluable.

Becky Chilcott and Alexis Snell for their work on the cover. I loved it from the very first draft, and I feel very lucky

to have such talented people produce the artwork for my book!

Alice Natali and Clementine Gaisman from the ILA team for working tirelessly to introduce Mara and Torniv to the readers in the wider world.

My friends all over the world, who, thanks to the wonders of modern technology, I always feel close to, no matter the distance.

And finally, thank you, reader, for picking up this book.

GLOSSARY

❀ **Baba** – An old woman/crone

❀ **Babcha** – Grandma

❀ **Boyars** – Members of the old aristocracy in Russia

❀ **Gontova/Gontovy/Gontovna** – Slavic surnames have different endings for the different members of the family. "Gontovy" is for the man. "Gontova" means "the wife of Gontovy" and "Gontovna" means "the daughter of the Gontov family"

❀ **Izba** – Room (often the largest room in a wooden house)

❀ **Kokoshnik** – An elaborate headdress

❀ **Lament** – A song or poem of grief

❀ **Mamusha** – Mummy

❀ **Marushka** – Diminutive of "Mara". Many Slavic languages have special forms to change the meaning of a name or any noun really, to express the emotions accompanying the person/word. In this case it could be translated as "dear little Mara"

❀ **Moya zabka** – My little frog (a term of endearment)

❀ **Slonechko moye** – My little sun (a term of endearment)

❀ **Sniezinka** – A snowball

❀ **Synek** – Son (diminutive form, literally means "little son")

❀ **Tsarevic** – A prince

❀ **Voz** – A horse-drawn cart

IF YOU LIKED THIS,
YOU'LL LOVE . . .

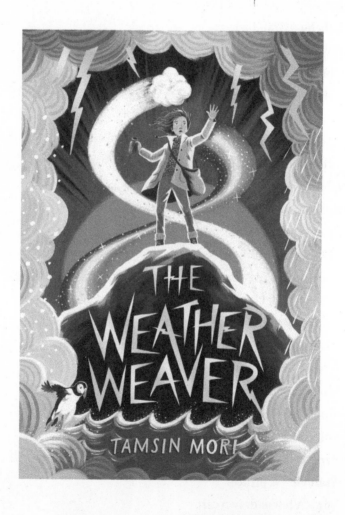